JINA

A CHRISTIAN ROMANTIC SUSPENSE

OATH OF HONOR

LAURA SCOTT

CHAPTER ONE

Tactical police officer Jina Wheeler threw her gym bag over her shoulder and walked into the crisp autumn night air. There was nothing better than a hard-core, sweaty round of kickboxing to end the day.

When Jina had first joined the mixed martial arts gym four months ago, she'd been irritated when the guys had instantly hit on her. When flat refusals didn't work, she'd invited them to a sparring match. After putting several of them down on the mat in record time, they'd backed off. Now they let her work out in peace.

There was one guy, Cole, whom she saw frequently but who had never once approached her. She only knew his name because Mike, the gym owner, called out to him one day. The two guys were apparently on a first-name basis. Cole was probably married, yet she'd caught him watching her a time or two. Looking wasn't against the law, and maybe he was just curious about how she'd come out on top over the guys.

It didn't matter; she wasn't interested. Okay, she was a little curious about him, but she had no intention of acting on it. Her experience with men wasn't good. During high school, she'd dealt with a creepy stalker, then in college, she'd been attacked and sexually assaulted. On top of that, she and Jaxon Palmer had been best friends in high school, but he'd gotten upset when she'd refused to relocate to Nashville with him. She hadn't understood why Jaxon had thought she'd leave her sister behind in the first place, and after she'd flat-out refused, she'd never heard from him again.

Proof that men weren't worth the time or energy it took to find a good one in a sea of losers. Not to mention, most of the guys she met were put off by a woman who could fight and shoot better than they could.

A rueful smile tugged at the corner of her mouth as she headed toward her car, a boxy black Jeep Wrangler. The early September weather was nice enough that she still had the top off, making it easy to toss her gym bag into the back seat. Just because half the members of her tactical team were settling down and getting married didn't mean she planned to follow suit. She was fine on her own 99 percent of the time. She chose to ignore the other 1 percent that she found herself envious of her younger sister Shelly's life.

From somewhere behind her, a car door slammed. She glanced back over her shoulder, cop instincts going on full alert, then relaxed when she saw a pair of headlights flash on. Just someone else leaving the gym.

As she wrenched open her driver's side door, she caught a glimpse of a shadow moving along the side of the building. A man? Adrenaline still zipped through her veins from her strenuous workout, and she quickly reached across the front seat to pull her service weapon from the glove box.

A nanosecond later, the sharp crack of gunfire echoed through the night. There was no metallic ping of her vehicle being hit. She ducked, her fingers closing around the handle of her gun. In a smooth movement, she held the weapon in a two-handed grip while crouching alongside her Jeep, wishing she had the top on for added cover.

Who was the perp trying to hit? It couldn't be her, unless the guy had terrible aim.

A second crack of gunfire ripped through the night. Okay, now she was getting mad. This guy was going to hurt some innocent bystander if he didn't knock it off.

"Police!" she shouted. "Drop your weapon!"

Listening intently, she heard nothing but silence. Hopefully, Duncan, the new second-shift gym manager, would call 911. She peeked up from behind the Jeep, scanning the area next to the building.

Spying a flash of movement, she darted out from behind the car and ran across the parking lot. Pounding footsteps indicated the perp was running away.

No way would she let him escape!

"Stop! Police!" she shouted again, putting on a burst of speed. When she reached the corner of the building, though, she paused, as there was no one in sight.

The gym was located on a mostly empty stretch of road, with a long, wooded area a few yards behind it. Rushing into the possible line of fire wouldn't be smart, but she really wanted to get this guy.

"Jina? Are you okay?"

She froze at the unknown male voice behind her. Then she whirled to face the new threat. Two perps working together? Wait, that didn't make sense as this one had called her by name.

"Duncan?" She tried to see the bearded man through the darkness. "Is that you?"

"No, my name is Cole. I heard gunfire. I'm hoping Duncan is inside calling the police."

Cole knew her name? For some reason that knocked her off balance. "I'm fine, except for the fact that the shooter is getting away."

"Let's split up and see if we can grab him." Cole came up to stand beside her, and she noticed he was also carrying a gun. "You head right; I'll go left."

"Got it." She didn't need to be asked twice. Darting across to the woods to the right, she heard Cole doing the same to the left. His movements and actions screamed cop, which shouldn't have been surprising.

Several cops hung out at Mike's MMA gym. Her included.

The woods stretched along the length of the building but weren't deep. She quickly found herself in another parking lot of what appeared to be a strip mall of small businesses. Glancing to her left, she noticed Cole had come out of the woods several yards away as well.

Without saying anything, he waved his gun toward the strip mall. She nodded and headed that way, staying to the right. Upon reaching the back side of the mall, she narrowed her gaze at a parked dark SUV. The lights abruptly blinded her, and the driver hit the gas, going from zero to thirty miles per hour before she could blink.

She wanted to fire at the vehicle but couldn't be certain the driver was their shooter. Until he continued heading straight for her. She was forced to dive to the ground, tucking and rolling to avoid behind hit. Lifting her head, she tried to get the license plate, but the vehicle was already gone.

Swallowing a silent curse—she'd given up swearing since joining Rhy's tactical team—she pushed herself up to her feet just as Cole rushed toward her. "What happened?"

"He tried to run me over." She couldn't help feeling disgusted with her poor performance. "I should have fired first and asked questions later."

"No, you did the right thing," Cole assured her. "Firing at the wrong perp would have required a ton of paperwork."

She couldn't hold back a bark of laughter, because he was right. If she had been wrong about the driver, she would have been stuck in a local police station for the rest of the night. "Yeah, well, I must be losing it because I didn't get the license plate either."

"I don't think there was one, or it was covered in some way." He raked a gaze over her. "You're not hit?"

"No. And I don't think my Jeep was struck either." She turned to head back through the trees to the gym parking lot. It seemed to be taking the local police a while to respond. "Guess it's a good thing the guy is a lousy shot."

"Yeah." Cole fell into step beside her. "Any idea about who wants to hurt you?"

She shot him a sidelong glance. "As a cop, I make a lot of enemies. But no one specific comes to mind."

"You work out of the Seventh Precinct in Milwaukee, right?" Cole asked.

She narrowed her gaze. "And you know that how?"

"Mike mentioned it," Cole said with a shrug. "I'm a detective with the Peabody Police Department."

"I figured you were a cop." She didn't like hearing he'd asked around about her. But she wasn't a scared teenager trying to get rid of a creepy stalker or college student fighting off a rapist anymore. She could handle herself in a way she hadn't been able to before.

When they reached the gym building, the wail of sirens

indicated the cops were finally on the way. Since she couldn't leave, she pulled out her phone and used the flashlight app to scan for shell casings. Cole did the same thing, spreading out from where she was working.

"Found one," she said, crouching down to look at it more closely. "Probably a .38."

"Good eye. And here's the second one." Cole gestured to the casing just three feet away. "Same caliber. Looks like he was moving back when he fired the second time."

"Or he moved closer after missing the first shot." She glanced at him. "Either way, he was pretty far off the mark."

"That's a blessing," Cole said with a nod. "I'm glad no one was hurt." Then he straightened as two uniformed Brookland police officers came toward them. He stepped forward to introduce himself. "I'm Peabody Detective Cole Roberts, and this is Officer Jina . . ." He arched a brow. She was glad Mike hadn't given out her last name.

"Officer Jina Wheeler with MPD." Gesturing toward the ground, she added, "We found two shell casings from the location from where the perp fired at me."

"Maybe you should start at the beginning," the older of the two men said. "Who was shooting at you?"

"I have no idea. Maybe a disgruntled perp I put away at some point." She went on to give her statement as succinctly as possible. To his credit, Cole didn't interrupt. After she'd finished, he added his version of the incident.

"This guy shot at you twice, then tried to run you over?" the younger officer asked.

"Yep. I wish I could give you a plate number, but all I know for sure is that the vehicle was a dark-colored SUV. Not a Jeep, the front grill was different, but maybe a Honda or a Hyundai?" She glanced at Cole for his input.

He nodded. "Pretty sure it was a Honda. The license plate was either missing or covered."

The cops asked several more questions before letting them go. Jina headed toward her Jeep, then abruptly stopped as Cole joined her.

"Did you need something?" The statement came out more accusatory than she'd intended.

"No. I was just walking you to your car," he answered evenly.

"I'm a cop, Cole." She scowled. "I don't need a babysitter."

"Wasn't volunteering for that role. Just making sure there are no other surprises lurking nearby."

She crossed her arms over her chest. "Thanks for the assist, but I have it from here."

He held her gaze for a long moment. The fact that she remembered his eyes were a dark chocolate brown annoyed her. "Suit yourself."

It was on the tip of her tongue to tell him she always did suit herself rather than catering to the whims of others, but he chose that moment to turn to head back to the other side of the parking lot.

Let him go, she told herself sternly. This little interlude was nothing special. He'd backed her up tonight the same way any other cop would have done. The way she would have done if the situation had been reversed.

She took a moment to double-check that no one was hidden inside the Jeep before sliding in behind the wheel. Tucking her weapon under her thigh, she started the engine and drove out of the parking lot. The wind pulled strands of her long blond hair from its ponytail, and she tucked them behind her ear as she covered the distance to her upper-level flat located five miles away.

The brown and tan two-story brick building was owned by Mr. Glen Gleason, an elderly widower. After a few months of watching him struggle, she'd taken over doing the yard work and snow removal without accepting a break on her rent. As a result, Mr. Gleason hadn't raised her monthly payments in over two years. The arrangement suited her just fine.

Still wondering about the shooter, she pulled into the garage. Mr. Glen parked on the other side but didn't do a lot of driving except to church and the grocery store. She tucked her weapon into her waistband, grabbed her gym bag, and made her way toward the side entrance that led to her upper-level flat. Mr. Gleason was hard of hearing, so she didn't worry about waking him up at this late hour of midnight.

But when a pair of headlights pierced the darkness out front, she paused, reaching for her gun. If this guy had shown up for round two, she'd enjoy taking him down.

Letting her bag slip to the ground, she darted toward the street. The vehicle abruptly veered away from the curb, tires squealing.

She stared after the disappearing car, noting again the absence of a license plate. Despite her confidence in her abilities, a chill snaked down her spine.

It wasn't good that this guy knew where she lived. The memory of how she'd shot and mostly missed her stalker nearly twelve years ago flashed in her mind.

No way would she miss this time. If this guy showed up again, she'd drop him where he stood without a smidgen of remorse.

CHASING a shooter had not been how Cole had planned to end his night, but he had to admit that meeting Jina was interesting.

He drove to her place, mentally preparing himself for her anger. He'd planned to interview her after their workout, but the shooter had put a dent in that plan. Chatting with her while cops swarmed the area hadn't been an option either. His only choice was to head out to her place so they could speak in private.

He knew her address and her last name, even though he'd pretended otherwise. He hadn't wanted to open that can of worms in front of the other officers.

She hadn't reacted to his being a Peabody Detective, but maybe she'd learned of his vocation through Mike. The same way he'd learned about her. At least initially.

Before the cold case had reared its ugly head. Literally.

He pulled into the driveway of the two-story brick building, frowning when he noticed Jina was still outside, holding her weapon in hand. Concerned, he quickly pushed out of the driver's side door. "What's wrong? Did the perp return?"

"What are you doing here?" she asked with a scowl. "How did you find me?"

"Why are you standing there holding your piece?" he countered. "I want to know if that guy showed up again."

She stared at him with deep suspicion for a long minute before gesturing to the street. "Maybe. I noticed a parked car at the curb. The lights flicked on, then the driver peeled away less than a minute before you showed up."

He didn't like the sound of that. "And you have no idea who might be holding a grudge against you?"

"No. Do you remember every perp you put behind

bars? That's an impossible task." Her eyes narrowed. "Now it's your turn. Why are you here?"

He stifled a sigh, realizing she had a right to be concerned. "I wanted to talk to you without an audience."

She arched a brow. "Okay, talk."

It wasn't easy to switch gears, but he had a job to do. And he wasn't about to let a beautiful face distract him. "I'm a detective with the Peabody Police Department."

"Yeah. You mentioned that." She stood her ground, not giving an inch. Obviously, she had no intention of inviting him in for a soft drink.

"I'm working a cold case." He watched her closely, but her expression didn't change. "You're aware of the new subdivision going in on the far west side of the Peabody? Not far from Surrey?"

A flicker of surprise crossed her features, but it was gone in an instant. "No, I wasn't aware of that. I thought Peabody had been subdivided to death."

Interesting turn of phrase, he thought with a cynical smile. Death in the subdivision was exactly why he was here. "Yes, it mostly has. This is the last ten acres of land that's being developed. You know the area, don't you?" He paused, waiting for her to acknowledge that, but she simply stared at him without saying a word. He should have expected her to be well-versed about how to respond during a police interview. "Our records show that the Wheeler family owned a sixty-acre farm in Peabody. Elias and Marsha Wheeler were your parents, right?"

"Yes, that's true," she answered without hesitation.

"You and your sister, Shelly, grew up there. Until your parents sold the property. The house was bulldozed, and the land was sold off in ten-acre parcels."

She shrugged. "Yes. Shelly and I grew up there, and my parents did sell the farm after my dad's heart attack. He died two years later, so it turned out to be a good thing for my mom. I'm not sure why that matters now. We haven't lived on the farm in years."

"I'm aware your sister lives in Madison with her husband," he said with a nod. "I plan to talk with her too."

Anger flashed in her eyes. "Why? Shelly is pregnant; there's no reason to upset her. I just told you we haven't lived there in years."

"Eleven years give or take a few months," he agreed. "Why would talking to me upset your sister?"

She flushed. "I'm a cop, and you're a detective. I assume some crime has taken place that has brought you here, dredging up the past. Shelly had a miscarriage last year and is in the early months of her pregnancy. I don't want her to be overly upset."

Was there more to her concern? "I promise I won't stress your sister."

She looked like she wanted to argue but didn't.

After another pause, he decided they'd tap-danced enough. "I need to know if you know anything about a male body being buried on the farm."

Something subtle flashed in her eyes. Alarm? Fear? Worry? "Are you serious? I hadn't heard anything about that."

"You're sure?"

She lifted her chin. "Yes. I don't know anything about a dead body. Sounds like you believe this man was the victim of a crime." When he nodded without expounding on why that was, she asked, "Do you know anything else about the victim? How old he was? How long he's been buried there?"

He couldn't fault her for asking the same questions he would have. Yet he sensed she was more than a little curious about what had been found. Maybe because she was a cop, or because she knew more than she was letting on. "We're waiting for the ME to finish the forensic examination, but his initial assessment based on the degree of decomp of what was left of the clothing is that the body was underground for at least a decade, maybe longer."

This time she didn't react at all. "Wow, I guess that explains why you're here asking me questions about where I grew up. I'm sorry, but I don't know anything about the dead man. I wish I could help, but I'm sure that poor guy was put there after we moved."

Maybe, maybe not. "You are helping by talking to me." He wondered again why she'd bristled about his interviewing her sister. "I have a few more questions if that's okay."

"I'll do my best." Her smile came across as forced.

"There was a young man who went missing about twelve years ago. Do you remember anything about that?"

"Missing?" She frowned, looking confused. "I don't remember anything about a missing person. Granted, twelve years ago I was only seventeen, but I believe I would have remembered something like that. A missing person would be a hot topic of conversation around town at the time."

He tried to gauge if she was being truthful. She didn't look as if she were hiding anything, but it was dark, and he found it difficult to read nuances in her expression. "The missing man's name was Bradley Crow, and he would have been twenty years old back then." He paused, waiting for a response. When she remained silent, he asked, "Can you tell me if that name sounds familiar?"

"Bradley Crow," she repeated, her brow furrowed. "No, sorry. That name doesn't sound at all familiar. I attended Peabody High School, and I think I'd remember someone with the last name of Crow."

He'd convinced himself that her path had crossed with Brad Crow's at one point or another, but maybe not. He tried to give her the benefit of the doubt. "He was probably a few years ahead of you in school." Cole didn't add that Bradley had been a high school dropout working for a local pub owned by his parents before he disappeared. And that his parents hadn't even reported him missing until after he had been gone for a full three months.

He was here to interview Jina, not the other way around.

"Yeah, well, my high school days were a long time ago." She uncrossed her arms as if she were feeling less defensive. "Sorry I can't help."

He prided himself on his ability to read people, but Jina was doing an admirable job of maintaining her composure while being grilled about a dead body found on her parents' farmland.

Or covering up the truth. It was annoying that he wasn't sure which.

"Do you remember anything strange going on back then?" He searched her gaze in the darkness. "Anything that, looking back, raises a red flag?"

She looked thoughtful for a moment, then shook her head. "No. Farming wasn't going well for my parents. Like I said, my dad had a heart attack, so the moment I graduated from high school, they sold the property. Some houses were already going in back then, so the land was purchased at a premium. They moved to a smaller house outside of Madison. It wasn't that much longer before my dad died. My mom was a nurse and worked at the health center. I headed off to college, and Shelly finished high school there."

"I see." He'd wondered if her parents had sold the place because of some mishap with Brad Crow. Maybe the stress of killing a kid who was bothering his beautiful daughters had caused her father's heart attack. But if that was the case, he'd need to come at this from another angle. Jina wasn't giving him anything to go on. "I noticed your mom passed away five years ago."

"Yes. She had pancreatic cancer." Jina's expression reflected her grief and sorrow. "It's just me and Shelly now."

He nodded, and when she didn't say anything more, he decided to let it go. "Well, that's all I have for tonight, but I may have to stop by to talk to you again."

"I understand," Jina said. "I know how police investigations work."

Yeah, and that was exactly what he was afraid of. "Thanks again. I appreciate your help."

He was about to turn back to his car, when she asked, "How did your vic die?"

He glanced at her over his shoulder. "Why do you ask?"

"Just cop curiosity." Was it his imagination, or did she sound nervous? "You must have found something that indicated he was a victim of a crime."

He hesitated, tempted to simply walk away. But then he surprised himself by saying, "His skull was bashed in."

Her eyes widened with shock that appeared genuine. Or maybe that was wishful thinking on his part. "Really? That's awful. I can't believe some poor dead man was found on our old farm property."

Again, he wasn't sure if he was imagining things, but it seemed to him that Jina was relieved by the news.

As Cole slid behind the wheel of his SUV, he wondered if that was good or bad. Either way, he knew he'd be back to talk to her again.

Very soon.

CHAPTER TWO

A dead man was found on the old farm property. The immediate threat of the shooter showing up at her home paled in comparison to the news Detective Cole Roberts dropped on her like a bomb. She sat in her kitchen, reliving the interview. When he'd mentioned the dead guy, she'd momentarily feared the worst. That she had in fact killed the man who'd tried to climb into her bedroom window twelve years ago.

But she knew he'd run off, so they couldn't be one and the same. Yes, she had found a bit of a blood trail, but nothing significant. Not like an arterial bleed or anything like that.

And she absolutely had not bashed his head in.

That image brought back the incident in college when Rory Glick had tried to force himself on her. She had smashed her laptop computer against his head but hadn't killed him either. She'd reported that incident to the campus police who arrested him and took the computer in as evidence. Rory had done time in jail for two years before being released. A condition of his release was that he had to be listed on the sex offender website. The last time she'd checked, he was still in Tulsa, Oklahoma, where his parents lived.

Could he be the shooter? Not likely. He wouldn't know she was a cop. And really, why come after her all these years later?

Which brought her back to the dead guy who'd been found on her parents' property. She hadn't liked lying to Cole when he'd asked about anything strange happening back then. Maybe she should have told him about the stalker incident, but since she hadn't reported the case twelve years ago, giving out that information now would only make her look more guilty. Sure, she hadn't killed anyone other than in the line of duty; however, Cole would be forced to consider her a suspect.

A blemish on an otherwise spotless career.

No, she wasn't going to let that happen. Could her stalker have been this Bradley Crow guy who'd gone missing? If so, how? And why? She couldn't find a logical explanation, unless Crow had stalked some other girl whose father, brother, or boyfriend had smashed his skull. That was far more likely in the big scheme of things.

It was fruitless to wish she'd done something different back then. At seventeen, she hadn't understood how the legal system worked. She'd been afraid she'd be arrested. So she'd kept her mouth shut.

Had her stalker gone to the emergency department at the local hospital? She felt certain he hadn't because a gunshot wound would be an automatic report to the police. And surely he would have turned her in as trying to kill him. Unless he'd fabricated another story about how he'd been injured.

One thing was for sure, nobody had come to the farmhouse to interview her or her parents. Her parents hadn't been home that night anyway, so they were clueless.

But Shelly knew the truth.

Jina shot out of her chair to pace the room. She couldn't call Shelly now. Not only was it well past midnight, and her pregnant sister needed rest, but if Cole obtained a subpoena for her cell phone, the call at this hour right after her interview would only raise more questions.

A disposable phone might work, but Shelly's phone records would reveal the call too. Too risky. A better idea was to hop into her car and drive the eighty miles to Madison.

But that would mean missing work. She raked her hand through her hair and winced, hating the thought of disappointing her bosses Rhy and Joe, but it couldn't be helped.

Tactical team captain Rhy Finnegan and lieutenant Joe Kingsley were always good about supporting members of the tactical team when personal time was needed. She hadn't taken a vacation in over a year, so she doubted they'd deny her request.

But they might ask questions. Questions she wasn't ready to answer.

When joining the police academy, she'd answered honestly about not committing any crimes. And firing at a stalker climbing into her bedroom window who'd subsequently fled on foot wasn't exactly a crime. Yet she had covered up a potential crime against her and her role in scaring him off. At the time, she'd told herself it didn't matter.

Now she wasn't so sure. The one sticking point was that she had used her father's gun without permission. With a wince, she pressed her fingers into her temples. Her head was pounding, and not because of the kickboxing work out. For the first time in years, she felt unsure of herself.

She didn't much like it.

Blowing out a frustrated breath, she grabbed her key fob off the table. There was no point in sticking around here, driving herself crazy. She would drive to Madison now so she'd be at her sister's bright and early. She'd sleep in her car —it wouldn't be the first time—then first thing in the morning, she'd call Rhy to ask for time off.

As plans went, it wasn't stellar, but it was the best she could do. And hopefully getting out of town would confuse the gunman too.

Could the two incidents be connected? Nah, that made even less sense than Rory coming after her all these years later. She'd been targeted by gunfire prior to knowing about the dead guy. And she was annoyed that Cole had hung around the gym waiting for a chance to interview her. His watching her hadn't been out of any personal interest after all.

After taking the time to shower and change, she packed an overnight bag. Then tossed her laptop computer in, too, just in case. Over the past few months, her teammates had gotten into some dicey situations in which she'd helped facilitate keeping them safe. Based on the gunman who'd fired at her outside the MMA gym, it seemed to be her turn. It would be good to leave town for a few days.

The last thing she wanted was to put Mr. Glen in harm's way.

Tiptoeing down the stairs, she headed back outside. The half-moon hung low in the sky, but there was more than enough ambient light for her to see. Still, she scanned the area carefully as she made her way to the garage.

After she dealt with Cole and his intent to interview her

sister, she'd need to go back through her records to see which perp she'd put away over the past eight years may have recently been released. One of them had to be the shooter, although how he'd known she attended Mike's MMA gym was concerning. She usually kept an eye out for anything suspicious, but the shooter must have followed her to the gym at some point. And had followed her to the duplex too.

The timing of both incidents nagged at her. She headed out of Greenland to the interstate. She'd driven the trip to Madison and back dozens of times and had to admit there was something to be said for driving in the middle of the night. There was hardly any traffic, especially once she was outside the suburb areas of the city. *Smooth sailing*, she thought with a sense of relief. Then she saw the signs indicating the next two exits were for the town of Peabody.

And irritably, that made her think of Cole Roberts.

Tracking her down and asking questions about the time she'd lived on the farm was a routine part of the investigative process. It bothered her that she'd assumed he was just another member of the gym when he'd come there specifically to find her.

Then again, she'd first noticed him right after she'd joined the gym four months ago. He was good-looking, but that wasn't what had drawn her attention. She worked with good-looking guys every single day. The fact that he'd watched her with interest while staying away had piqued her interest. Stupid, really, since she still didn't know if he was married, engaged, or seeing someone special.

And now it didn't matter. As the detective interviewing her and her sister about a cold case, he was way off-limits.

How long ago had the dead body been found? It couldn't have been that long, or he'd have sought her out before now. She kicked herself for not digging into the details surrounding that discovery prior to hitting the road.

It wasn't like her to be so rattled. As one of the sharp-shooters for their tactical team, she was known to be cool under pressure. She really needed to pull herself together.

She took note of a pair of headlights behind her. Far enough away that she wasn't concerned. But then with slow persistence, the gap closed between them.

Her weapon was on her hip, but she didn't reach for it yet. It seemed highly unlikely the shooter was behind her, but she found herself easing off the gas, hoping the driver would pass her.

He didn't.

Tightening her grip on the steering wheel, she considered her options. Despite how she hadn't put the top back on the Jeep, she considered going off-road. But that meant exiting the interstate first.

Or maybe not. A quick glance confirmed she was on a stretch of the highway that was rural. Flanked by farm fields on either side, there wasn't any place to hide.

She slowed her speed again, forcing the driver behind her to do the same. Then she gunned the engine and abruptly switched lanes. It took a few minutes for the driver of the car to come up alongside her. Without glancing at him, she hit the brake hard enough to make her tires squeal in protest. As soon as he shot past her, she crossed back into the right lane and drove right off the interstate, heading straight into the farm field. There had been a barn off in the distance, and her hope was to get there before this guy could follow.

Hitting the phone button on her steering wheel, she called 911. Out in the middle of nowhere, the state patrol would have jurisdiction. She had little hope they'd get there in time, but she had to try.

"This is 911, what is your emergency?" a calm voice asked.

"MPD Officer Jina Wheeler reporting a car attempting to run me off the road. I'm—ah"—she tried to remember the last exit she'd passed—"I'm a few miles past Johnson Creek. Please send a patrol car to this location."

"Roger that, Officer, please stay on the line as I radio for backup."

Jina was too focused on the rocky terrain beneath the wheels of her Jeep to pay any attention to the dispatcher. Farm fields might look nice and flat from far away, but they rarely were. This field was full of soybean plants that she was ruthlessly trampling beneath the wheels of her Jeep in her effort to escape.

She didn't pray, but the thought crossed her mind. Mostly because her teammates would have done that if they were sitting beside her. Checking the rearview mirror, she saw the headlights of the pursuing vehicle had also headed out into the farm's field.

Persistent jerk, she thought darkly. She pressed harder on the accelerator, increasing her pace despite the way her four-wheel drive bucked and swayed over the uneven ground.

Relieved to see the driver drop back, she failed to notice the patch to her right where there were no soybean plants. Until her right tire struck the rock protruding from the earth with enough force to flip the Jeep upside down, making her teeth rattle. The airbag deployed, smashing her in the face.

Batting at the airbag, she hung there for a moment like an upside-down turtle. A sense of urgency had her reaching for the seatbelt. Bracing herself with one arm, she released the latch and managed to roll to the side rather than falling on her bruised face. Without hesitation, she crawled out of the Jeep and looked around for the car.

At first, she thought the vehicle had made it back to the interstate and drove away. Until she noticed the dark shape of the car sitting in the distance with the headlights off.

A shiver of apprehension snaked down her spine. Then a flash of anger hit hard. She eased her weapon from the holster and inched backward beneath the Jeep, using it as cover.

She stretched out on her belly, her arms outstretched and the barrel of her gun pointed at the car. She would have loved to pepper it with bullets, but the distance between them was roughly eighty yards.

Almost the length of a football field. She sincerely wished she hadn't left her sniper's rifle behind in her apartment. Normally, she took it everywhere, but she hadn't expected to need it at her sister's.

Now she was too far out of range for her handgun to even hit the perp's vehicle, much less render it useless.

But she could be patient.

Regardless of the red tape, if that idiot behind the wheel was the shooter and came any closer, she would shoot first and ask questions later.

———

UNABLE TO SLEEP after his less than satisfactory interview with Jina, Cole was listening to the police scanner when the 911 call came in. Hearing her name, he jumped off the sofa, quickly dressed, grabbed his weapon, and hit the door at a run.

Of course, Jina had headed to Madison, he thought with

a burst of annoyance. No doubt she'd wanted to be there when he arrived at her sister's place the following morning for the dreaded interview.

While he found the move on Jina's part to be highly suspicious, his immediate concern was her report of a vehicle trying to run her off the interstate. As it was now just past one o'clock in the morning, the only logical explanation was that the driver was the same shooter who had shown up at the gym.

As he took the exit onto the interstate, he thumped his fist on the steering wheel. He knew he should have stayed in his car outside her duplex.

Cole hit the switch to turn on the red and blue light strip along the back of his SUV and floored the gas pedal, racing as fast as he dared toward Johnson Creek. The state patrol would probably arrive first, but he didn't care. After the event barely an hour ago, he had a vested interest in this gunman too.

Not to mention his need to confront Jina over her late-night trek to her sister's place. For claiming not to know anything about the dead guy on her family's farmland, she was mighty determined to keep him from doing his job.

What was up with that anyway? Was she really concerned about her sister's delicate condition, or was there something else going on?

His gut was screaming at him that there was far more to this situation than Jina had admitted to knowing.

No more professional courtesy. After this latest stunt of hers, their next interview would be at the Peabody police station. And if Jina didn't come clean this time, he'd toss her in jail until she did.

Up ahead, bright red and blue lights from the state

patrol lit up the sky. He searched the right-hand side of the road for signs of Jina's Jeep Wrangler but didn't find it.

Until he glanced over at the farmer's field. His jaw dropped when he saw the four wheels of her Jeep pointing at the sky. His gut clenched with fear.

Was she hurt? Killed?

His previous annoyance vanished behind a wave of concern. She could play the tough cop all she wanted, but she was still flesh and blood. And being an expert in jujitsu and kickboxing didn't mean she could survive a car crash.

He pulled in behind the patrol car and jumped out. There was no sign of the officer, so he shouted, "Jina!"

There was no response, which only made his pulse kick into high gear. Was she unconscious? There hadn't been a top on the Jeep an hour ago, and he prayed she hadn't been thrown from the vehicle.

As he grew closer to the upside-down car, Jina crawled out from beneath the Jeep and stood to face the patrol officer. A staggering relief hit hard, but he didn't slow his pace. "Jina, are you okay?"

"Cole?" She couldn't have looked more surprised to see him. "What are you doing here?"

"I heard the call come through the scanner." He raked his gaze over her, grateful there were no obvious signs of injury. Maybe some bruising to her face, but nothing too serious.

Thank you, Lord Jesus!

"And who are you?" the cop asked.

"Detective Cole Roberts." He felt slightly foolish for barreling out here like a bereaved boyfriend. "I'm with the Peabody Police Department."

"Detective Roberts was at the gym earlier when an unknown perp took two shots at me," Jina said, giving him an exasperated look. He belatedly realized she had an overnight bag slung over her shoulder. "I told you about that earlier. It looks like we're both working under the theory that these two incidents are related."

"What happened?" He gestured to the Jeep. "Did he ram into you?"

"No, I drove out here to avoid him." She scowled, clearly upset at the state of her vehicle. "I was watching him try to follow me across the farm field in the rearview mirror when my tire hit that giant bolder over there. That's what flipped me over."

"And where is that vehicle now?" the patrol officer asked. The guy's name tag indicated his last name was Parsons. "Are you sure you haven't been drinking?"

"I don't drink," Jina snapped, glaring at him. "If you want to do a field sobriety test, go ahead. As I already told you, the vehicle followed me only partway into the farmer's field. He must have realized he couldn't get all the way across without risking me firing at him, so he backed up and took off."

"Because he knows you're a cop," Parsons said with a frown.

"Yes, I identified myself as a police officer when he fired at me outside the gym." Jina looked annoyed with having to repeat herself. "Cole was there; he can corroborate my story."

"She absolutely identified herself as a cop," he repeated. "We tried to find him, but he managed to escape in an SUV after he tried to run her over." He glanced at Jina. "You think it was the same car we saw earlier?"

"It looked similar, yes, but I wasn't close enough to say for sure." She rubbed her left shoulder, and he imagined it was sore from the strap of the seat belt locking up across her chest. "When he was behind me, all I could see were his bright headlights."

"License plate?" Parsons asked.

"I didn't see one," Jina said.

Parsons looked at him, then at Jina. Apparently, the patrol officer had given up on the idea Jina had driven out into the farmer's field and flipped her Jeep because she was under the influence. "I can try to issue a BOLO, but without any identifying marks . . ." His voice trailed off.

"No license plate should be enough for the guy to get pulled over," Cole said.

Jina snorted. "That hasn't stopped him yet."

Parsons seemed a bit out of his depth. Cole knew rookies often ended up working the graveyard shift, and based on the fact that the guy didn't look old enough to grow a beard, he figured Parsons to be a newbie.

"We can take it from here," Cole told the officer. "I don't think there's anything more you can do tonight, other than issuing the BOLO."

"Yeah, okay." Parsons looked relieved. Then he frowned. "What about the Jeep?"

"I need you guys to help me flip it back over." Jina eyed her vehicle critically. "If all three of us work on this side, we should be able to roll it back up on the wheels."

Parsons didn't look happy about that, but Cole nodded, knowing Jina was stronger than she looked. And he worked out on a regular basis too. "Let's do it."

Amazingly, they were able to flip the car onto its passenger side, then again upright on all four wheels. Jina eagerly climbed into the driver's seat and tried to start the engine.

There was a grinding sound, then nothing. She tried

again with the same result. He was no mechanic, but obviously, the car wasn't going anywhere tonight.

"I'll drive you home," he offered. "You need a tow truck. The windshield is shattered, and you probably broke the front axle, anyway, after hitting that rock." He didn't want to add that the insurance company would likely total the vehicle.

"Yeah." Dejected, she slid out of the seat.

"Let's go." He gestured for her to take the lead.

"Ah, Detective Roberts? I need your phone number," Parsons said. "For my report."

He gave the rookie his office number at the Peabody PD. Then the three of them crossed the farmer's field. At about eighty yards from where Jina's car was located, she stopped to examine the ground with her phone flashlight.

"Now what are we looking for?" He scanned the area too. "Did he shoot at you?"

"No, he was too far away. I was hoping he would come close enough so I could nail him, but he didn't." She continued scanning the ground, then dropped to one knee. "Here, two sets of tire tracks. Mine and his."

"I see them." He glanced at Parsons who took out his phone to take pictures. "She was right about the car following her."

"Yeah. I'll—uh—add this to my report." Parsons looked a little embarrassed for doubting Jina in the first place. As he should.

After a few more minutes of examining the ground, Jina stood and nodded at Parsons. "Thanks for your help."

"No problem." Parsons climbed the embankment toward his patrol car. "Take care."

"I'll try," Jina muttered, mostly under her breath. "Although it would be nice to know who this joker is."

"Did you notice anyone following your Jeep from your place?" he asked.

"No, and I was watching for a tail." She rubbed her sore shoulder again. "The interstate was mostly deserted, which caused me to let my guard down. I honestly wasn't expecting the shooter to show. Even when I saw the head-lights of his car coming up behind me, I slowed down, assuming he'd pass me by. Only he didn't."

He hated to imagine what might have happened if Jina hadn't driven her Jeep across the farmer's field. "I take it you didn't see his face?"

"No." She scowled again. "Although there is a suspect I should have considered earlier."

His interest peaked. "Oh yeah? Who?"

"Guy by the name of Rory Glick. His last-known address is in Tulsa, Oklahoma, so it didn't occur to me until tonight that he might have come seeking revenge."

"Revenge over what exactly?"

"He tried to rape me until I slammed him in the head with my computer. He was arrested and did two years in prison. He was released too early for my peace of mind, his lawyer argued he was drunk and wasn't thinking clearly, but the fact that my clothes were ripped proved otherwise." She shrugged. "One condition of his release was that his name was placed on the sexual offender registry."

He hated thinking about Jina suffering a sexual attack. No wonder she'd put so many of the gym rats at Mike's down on the mat. He'd silently cheered her on, and now he knew why she was so determined to stick up for herself. "I'm sorry you had to go through that."

"I'm fine." She said the words carelessly, but he suspected those moments before she'd gotten a hold of the laptop had been terrifying. "What doesn't make sense is why Rory would come after me nine years later? He'd attended the University of Wisconsin in Madison, same as I did, but he was from Oklahoma. How could he have found me at Mike's?" She waved a hand at her Jeep. "And again tonight?"

"Those are good questions." He filed the name Rory Glick in the back of his mind for later. The gym shooting had not taken place in his jurisdiction, but that wasn't going to stop him from looking into what the sexual predator had been up to. "We can work on that later. For now, let's get out of here."

"Okay." She opened the passenger door and tossed her overnight bag onto the floor.

Seeing it reminded him of her intent to talk to her sister before he could. "Taking a trip?"

She flushed, her gaze sliding from his. "Yep."

"Give it up, Jina," he said in a clipped tone. "Don't lie to me. I know you were heading to your sister's house in Madison when this guy caught up with you."

"So what?" Jina shrugged as if she took middle of the night trips to see her pregnant sister every day. "I'm worried about Shelly. She's barely twelve weeks along in her pregnancy. I told you I wanted to be there to support her through this."

"No, you asked me why I'd bother to talk to her at all," he corrected. "Tell me the truth. Do you know Bradley Crow?"

"No, I don't." She spoke with confidence. "I meant to look him up on the computer but forgot. Why don't you show me a picture? Maybe I'll recognize him."

He hesitated, then pulled out his cell phone. Thumbing the screen, he brought up Bradley Crow's school picture. It was the only one he had of the guy. "This was taken his junior year."

As she looked at the screen, he could almost see the wheels turning in her mind, imagining where she may have seen him before. Then she handed the phone back. "Nope. I don't recognize him."

"I don't believe you." He slid the phone into his pocket.

"Believe what you want," she shot back. "Doesn't matter to me."

He waited until they were settled in the front seat and back on the road before turning to her. "You can come clean now or spend the night in jail. Your choice." He gestured to the interstate stretched out before them. "You have until we reach the Peabody city limits to decide."

She didn't answer, sitting back against her seat and staring straight out the windshield as if he didn't exist.

He suppressed a sigh. It was going to be a long twenty miles.

CHAPTER THREE

Jina tried to think of a way out of this mess. Cole didn't have much to hold her on, but she wasn't keen on being put through the system. There had been something about Bradley Crow's eyes that had bothered her, but the rest of his face had not looked familiar. Maybe her imagination was running rampant. Her stalker had always worn a hoodie and had a shock of curly dark hair hanging low on his forehead. There wasn't a lock of dark hair on his forehead in the picture of Bradley Crow. In truth, she'd only gotten a few glimpses of her stalker's face, only seeing him from afar.

At first, she hadn't thought much about seeing him lurking outside her school, then at the custard stand where she'd worked. But after a few weeks, she'd grown suspicious.

Her memory of the guy was that he was short, maybe five nine or ten, had a lean, lanky frame, and slinked around with his head down. She'd found him odd, but not in a threatening manner. Mostly like a nerd who had no idea how to talk to girls. Which was fine with her, as she wasn't interested. She had mentioned him to Jaxon as he'd worked at the custard stand with her, and her friend hadn't seemed overly concerned about hoodie guy either.

Now that she thought about it, she hadn't seen her hoodie stalker after she'd taken that shot at him. At the time, she'd assumed she'd scared him off and that was the end of that.

Now she had no idea what to think.

"The Peabody exit is in two miles," Cole said, breaking the silence.

She swallowed a curse. Keeping her promise not to swear with Cole around was difficult. The man was beyond annoying.

As much as she hated to admit it, he wasn't giving her much of a choice.

"Fine. There was one suspicious incident from twelve years ago." She didn't look at him as she spoke. "But I don't believe Bradley Crow is the guy involved."

"Involved in what?" He sounded irritable, and she supposed she couldn't blame him.

"I had a stalker incident my senior year of high school." She hated talking about her past. Having a stalker, then being nearly raped only made her appear weak. In the years since, she'd prided herself on being strong and capable, which had earned her the position as the tactical team sharpshooter. "I don't know his name. He wore a hoodie and slinked around, popping up everywhere I went."

There was a long pause as he considered that. "Okay, so what happened? Did you report him to the police?"

Here was where things got dicey. "Not exactly. For one thing, Peabody didn't have a robust police department like they do now. I believe we shared a police department with Surrey. And for weeks the guy didn't do anything other than watch me from a distance."

Cole's fingers tightened on the steering wheel as if he was losing his patience. "But he didn't stop at watching you," he finally said.

"No. He showed up one Saturday night at our house. My parents were gone, and Shelly and I were home alone." She risked a sideways glance at him. His grim expression didn't reveal his thoughts. "It was late, maybe eleven o'clock at night, when I heard a strange noise. I grabbed my father's handgun and went to investigate. When I looked in my bedroom, the hoodie guy was climbing in through the window."

"He entered your house?" Now Cole turned to look at her in shock. "What did you do?"

"I shouted that I had a gun. He didn't move, so I fired at him." She gripped her hands together in her lap. "That worked; he turned and ran away."

"You missed?" Cole asked.

"Not exactly." She cleared her throat. "I think I hit his arm or shoulder. There was blood on the right side of my window frame and another spattering on the ground outside. I followed the blood trail across the grass, then it disappeared near the road. It wasn't nearly enough blood to indicate I'd hit an artery or anything like that."

"And that's when you reported the incident to the police?"

She didn't answer, earning another scathing look.

"Unbelievable," he muttered. "You didn't call the police about a man trying to climb into your bedroom window."

"No. I was worried I'd get in trouble for firing my father's gun. Besides, I didn't see him lurking around after that, so I was pretty sure I'd scared him away." She forced a smile. "Mission accomplished."

His jaw tensed, and it was a long moment before he spoke. "Are you absolutely sure this stalker of yours doesn't look anything like Bradley Crow?"

It was her turn to battle a flash of anger. "I was seventeen, Cole. I never saw his face up close and personal. It was dark in my room, which is likely why he'd tried to get in that way. I only remember he wore a hoodie and had dark, thick, curly hair that covered his forehead." She wasn't going to mention the weird eyes. "So no, I can't say anything for certain. Except that the last time I saw him, he was running away. And for sure I didn't bash him in the head, so I doubt he's your dead guy."

"Someone else may have bashed him in the head," Cole said in a tight voice. "Did it ever occur to you that you may not have been his only victim? That he might have done the same thing to someone else?"

To her shame, she hadn't. But she did her best to squelch the flash of guilt. "I never heard anyone mentioning it, but anything's possible. However, after shooting and hitting him in the arm, I was convinced he'd keep his hands to himself."

Cole didn't respond to that. After a moment, she noticed he'd taken the Peabody exit. A flash of alarm hit hard.

"What are you doing? I'm cooperating, aren't I?"

"Yeah, but you can't go back to your place, the gunman knows where you live." His voice was calm. "You can sleep on my couch if you like. Or you can go to a hotel."

"How about none of the above?" She resisted the urge to punch him in the arm. "I can take care of myself. Besides, the shooter probably won't try again tonight. For all he knows, I'm still stranded out in the farm field."

"Oh really?" He scowled. "You think he's satisfied having missed you twice now? Or is it three times?"

"I'm not sure he was the same one outside my place, so that doesn't count." Why was she arguing with him? It was bad enough he'd derailed her plan to go to Madison; under no circumstances was she going to sleep on his sofa. Or anywhere else for that matter. "Drop me off at my place. Or I'll just grab a rideshare to get home. I won't use any lights, which should convince the perp I'm not there."

There was still the possible threat to Mr. Glen, but it was late enough now that she hoped she wouldn't have to worry about that until morning. Especially if she was able to sneak into the house in the dark.

The events of the past few hours were catching up to her. Every muscle in her body ached with a vengeance. Her soreness from the three kickboxing matches had been aggravated by rolling the Jeep. Her left shoulder throbbed from where the seatbelt had held her in place while she hung upside down.

Taking a hot bath in the dark wouldn't be so bad. All she had to do was avoid falling asleep.

"I'm going on record in saying this is a bad idea," Cole said, interrupting her thoughts. "But if you insist, I'll take you home."

"I insist." She rested her head back on the cushion, belatedly adding, "Thanks."

They traveled the rest of the way in silence. Only when he pulled up to the curb, a full block from her duplex, did he ask, "Do you want me to pick you up in the morning?"

"For what?" Then she realized what he meant. "You're still going to Madison to interview my sister?"

"Yes. As a courtesy, I'll take you with me as long as you don't get in my way." He turned to face her. "I'm not the bad guy here. I'm just trying to find answers to who this dead guy is and how he got buried on your old family farm. Bradley Crow might not be your stalker, but I still need to do my job."

He was going out of his way to be nice, and most cops would not allow her to tag along on an interview. Biting back a sharp retort, she nodded and forced a smile. "That would be great. Thanks."

"It's past two in the morning now, so we won't hit the road until nine. If that works for you?"

"I'll be ready." She pushed open her passenger-side door. "Thanks again."

"You're welcome."

Sliding out of the vehicle, she looked around, then made her way swiftly to the duplex, keeping in the shadows as much as possible. As she silently entered the house, she realized she hadn't called for a tow truck. Swallowing a groan, she decided to wait until tomorrow morning.

Confessing her role in shooting the stalker hadn't been as bad as she'd feared. Yes, Cole had been annoyed with her actions, but he hadn't hammered her over the head about her decision not to go to the authorities.

Yet as she crawled into bed, foregoing the soak in the tub, she knew there would be more to come. Cole might be understanding, but she doubted the rest of the Peabody Police Department would feel the same way.

She forced herself to relax her sore muscles, doing her best not to fixate on the sick feeling in her gut that the mistakes of her past were coming back to bite her in the butt.

THE FOLLOWING MORNING, Cole rubbed his eyes, waiting for the coffee to brew wondering why on earth he'd agreed to bring Jina along while he interviewed her sister, Shelly Strom.

If his boss found out, he'd be toast. Especially if it turned out Jina's stalker was the dead guy.

He didn't think she'd lie about not being the one who'd bashed the dead guy's head in. After all, she was a cop too. Sworn to uphold the law and protect the public. He believed she'd fired her father's gun to scare him off, and really, it was a miracle she hadn't killed the guy considering the close range.

Mike Pulaski, the MMA gym manager, had told him about Jina's role as a sharpshooter for the tactical team. Apparently, she'd honed those skills after the stalker incident. After being a victim twice in a matter of years, he completely understood why she'd chosen the path of becoming a cop.

He even admired her for overcoming her past, but that didn't mean her role in his investigation didn't complicate things.

And who was this shooter anyway? He'd dug into Rory Glick's past, found the guy on the sexual offender registry, and had read the police report. It had given him a surge of satisfaction to learn Glick had suffered a minor concussion from being struck with the laptop.

Score one for Jina.

There was no indication that Glick was in Wisconsin, but he would place a call to the Tulsa PD later to see if they'd had any trouble with the guy. He didn't think there was enough evidence leaning toward Glick being the shooter to justify a search warrant for his phone or credit card records.

Had Jina's old stalker returned? But much like suspecting Glick of being the shooter, why would the hoodie stalker show up to tail Jina after all this time? Twelve long years after the fact?

Especially since she hadn't called the police to have him arrested? In Cole's mind, the guy had gotten off easy with a minor injury. Why seek revenge now?

Belatedly realizing the coffee was finished, he poured himself a cup and returned to his kitchen table. He jiggled the mouse to bring the computer to life.

Maybe the motive was simple rather than complicated. Jina was stunningly beautiful, probably the most gorgeous woman he'd ever met. Certainly, she'd turned every guy's head at the MMA gym. Maybe one of those two guys, Glick or the stalker, was just angry that she'd jilted them—shooting one and clubbing the other with a computer.

Anger and resentment could fester over the years.

Maybe one or both had been in jail for a while. And it was only once they'd been released that they'd come after her.

There was also a third possible scenario. That one of Jina's more recent arrests had gotten out of jail and was seeking payback.

Lots of suspects with few leads to go on. He didn't think the perp was a fellow cop because as Jina had pointed out, he was a lousy shot. She'd been standing by her Jeep in plain view when he'd fired his weapon.

No, more likely it was someone with a personal vendetta against her. Did that include any of the guys she ruthlessly put down on the mat at the gym? He hated to admit that these attacks against Jina were more likely to have stemmed from a more recent incident rather than something that had transpired years ago.

Thinking back, he hadn't noticed any of the gym rats mouthing off about her. At least, not while he was around. He sent a quick text to Mike, briefly explaining the danger to Jina in case he was missing something.

Funny how he was driving himself crazy over a case that technically wasn't his. Better for him to stay focused on the skeletal remains that had been unearthed on the former Wheeler farm. Having an ID for their vic was the first step. Hopefully, he'd hear from the ME's office very soon. They had the fractured skull, and he had already asked for the jawbone and teeth to be compared with the missing Bradley Crow's dental records.

Glancing at his watch, he decided it was well past time to hit the shower. As a peace offering, he'd stop for breakfast sandwiches and more coffee on the way to Jina's. Despite knowing he shouldn't be bringing her along to his interview of her sister, he was looking forward to seeing her again.

As soon as the thought formed, he winced. Not good. Was he out of his mind? He'd lost his wife, Renee, three years ago and had no intention of going down that path again. So why was he suddenly interested in Jina? She might be pretty, but she was pricklier than a cactus.

Besides, beauty was only skin deep.

Yet there was no denying he was intrigued by the beauty queen who could hold her own against a bunch of gym rats.

Enough. He wasn't interested in Jina aside from getting information from her early years of living in Peabody. He'd grown up in Milwaukee, but Renee had lived in Peabody, so he'd transferred to the smaller and admittedly safer Peabody Police Department in part to make his wife happy. But now that he was working a cold case, he felt at a disadvantage. He hadn't lived in Peabody twelve years ago. Any input Jina and Shelly could provide, especially regarding the people who'd lived in the area back then, would be great.

The two sisters might be close, but they lived their own lives. Despite Jina's insistence to the contrary, he was banking on the possibility that Shelly would recognize Bradley Crow.

He dressed in what he considered his detective uniform —dress slacks, short-sleeved shirt, and a sport coat. The worst part about having a gold shield was dressing up. Give him the starchy police uniform any day.

After clipping his badge on his belt and sliding his .38 into the holster, he headed for the door. He'd sold the house he'd shared with Renee and bought this smaller place. At the time, he'd thought that moving would help him deal with the memories of their time together, but it hadn't.

Renee had remained in his heart. It was only within the past ten months or so that he'd realized she hadn't occupied his thoughts as much as she used to.

Giving himself a mental shake, he drove to the fast-food restaurant closest to Jina's duplex for their breakfast. Then he navigated the six blocks to reach her driveway.

Seeing the house in daylight, he noted the property was well maintained. He slid out from behind the wheel, leaving the food and coffee in the car. He headed to the side entrance, only to stop abruptly as Jina appeared. The same overnight bag from last night hung from her shoulder.

"Hey." She didn't smile, and from the weariness in her features, he guessed she hadn't slept well. "I saw you pull up."

"No worries." He tried not to be suspicious of her unwillingness to allow him into her personal space. "I stopped for breakfast sandwiches and coffee."

"You did?" Her blue eyes brightened as she smiled. "Thanks."

Ridiculously pleased by her response, and somewhat rattled over how striking she was when she smiled, he stepped back so she could come down the sidewalk. In contrast to his being on duty, she was dressed casually in blue jeans and a yellow T-shirt beneath a denim jacket. She wore her long hair down rather than in the usual ponytail. She also had her weapon clipped to her belt, and he assumed she didn't go anywhere without it.

He went around to open her passenger door. She arched a brow but didn't point out that she was perfectly capable of opening her own door. She dropped the bag on the floor and slid inside.

"The coffee smells great." She reached for the cup.

"Cream and sugar packets are in the door if you need them." He gestured to the side pocket.

"Nope. I'm good."

He couldn't help but smile as he closed her door and headed to the driver's seat. The pleasant interlude would only last until they reached Madison, as he assumed she would turn into a mamma bear protecting her cub once he started to interview Shelly.

He shifted into gear and backed out of the driveway. "Who owns the building?"

"Mr. Glen. He's a sweetheart." She sipped her coffee, then set it aside. "What's for breakfast?"

Before he could answer, his phone rang. He hesitated, then answered the call from Mike Pulaski. "Hey, Mike. I'm here with Jina."

"Really?" The gym owner sounded shocked. "I got your text and just wanted to assure you that I have not heard anyone mouthing off about Jina. But that may be because I made it clear for the guys to keep their thoughts to themselves. That if they didn't like getting their butt kicked by a woman, they should join another gym."

Jina turned to look at him with annoyance, then spoke. "Thanks, Mike, but to be clear, I never thought any of the guys at the gym would be angry enough to shoot me."

"I'm glad to hear that. I don't think so either," Mike said earnestly. "But I'm happy to help. Just let me know what you need."

"I will," Cole said. "Thanks again." He ended the call, prepared for Jina to snap at him. But when he glanced at her, she was frowning while rifling through the overnight bag. "What's wrong?"

"You're going to think I'm an idiot, but I forgot my phone." She shot him a chagrined look. "I left it on the charger in my kitchen. Sorry, but can we head back to the duplex?"

"Of course." He made a quick U-turn to retrace their path. "I'm glad to know you're human and not a Terminator."

"Haha, very funny. That Terminator movie is older than dirt." She ran her fingers through her hair. "Normally, I'm not this scattered."

"Like I said, it's nice to know you're human." He frowned as he noticed dark smoke trailing up to the sky. "Do you see that? Something is on fire."

"I see it." She craned her neck to get a better look. "It is autumn, could be someone burning leaves."

"Maybe, but the smoke is darker than I'd expect for that." He quickly turned left, heading to the duplex. The cloud of smoke grew larger and darker as they drove. A sliver of apprehension slid down his spine.

"Not leaves," Jina said in a terse tone, mirroring his thoughts. "Either a garage or a house is on fire."

Silently agreeing with her assessment, he pressed the call button on his steering wheel and spoke. "Call 911."

Seconds later, a woman answered the phone. "This is the 911 operator, please state your emergency."

"I'd like to report a fire. We're heading north on 120th Street." He glanced at the house numbers and rattled them off too.

"Yes, we have received several reports of a house fire in that area," the dispatcher said. "Please stay away from the property. I have dispatched fire responders who will be arriving shortly."

He ended the call without saying anything more. Two minutes later, he turned onto the street where Jina lived. His stomach clenched when he saw the two-story brown and tan duplex had black smoke pouring from the lower-level windows.

"Stop the car! Mr. Glen!" Jina pushed her car door open before he'd come to a complete stop. Then she sprinted toward the house.

"Wait! You can't go in there!" He killed the engine, then quickly followed her to the house, the thick black smoke already obscuring his vision. "Jina!"

She had stripped out of her denim jacket and wrapped it around her fist as she punched through a window that wasn't oozing smoke. After knocking all the shards of glass out of the way, she poked her head through the opening. "Mr. Glen! Mr. Glen, can you hear me?"

He lunged for her, grabbing her arm to prevent her from climbing into the house. The smoke made them cough. "Wait for the fire department," he urged between hacking breaths.

"No! I need to find Mr. Glen!" With a quick move, she twisted out of his grip and crawled in through the broken window.

He glanced over his shoulder. The wailing sirens said help was on the way, but there was no sign of the fire trucks yet. Muttering about stubborn women, he followed her inside, praying God would spare their lives, especially her landlord, Mr. Glen.

CHAPTER FOUR

Coughs racking her body, Jina was horrified she couldn't see anything through the thick haze of smoke. Stumbling through the living room, she called out to Mr. Glen until nothing more than a hoarse croak emerged.

"Jina!" She turned blindly when Cole grabbed her arm. "There's an older guy outside walking with a cane!"

Mr. Glen used a cane, but there were several older residents in this neighborhood. She didn't want to leave but somehow found herself back at the broken window with Cole at her side. Filling her lungs with fresh air, or at least somewhat fresher air than what was inside the house, she peered at the older man standing on the sidewalk.

Mr. Glen! He was safe! And for the first time in her life, she silently added, *Thank You, God.*

"Jina? What's going on?" She heard Mr. Glen's confused voice as Cole pushed her through the window.

Still coughing, she tumbled out of the house, then ran toward her landlord. "I'm glad you're okay," she said, wrapping her arms around the older man.

"I'm glad you are too," he said, patting her back. "How did the fire start? Did you burn something in the kitchen?"

"Not me. I wasn't here." She glanced briefly at Cole who'd come to stand beside them. "I was with Cole; we were coming back for my phone." She coughed again, then added, "I was worried you were still inside."

"We're glad you're not hurt," Cole added.

"I went out for my usual walk," Mr. Glen said, staring in shock at the burning home. "I don't understand how this happened."

She had a very bad feeling this was no accident. And if she hadn't come back for her phone, she wouldn't have known anything about it. Before she could ask Mr. Glen more questions, the sirens grew louder. Soon a long fire truck lumbered up the road toward the duplex, pulling to a stop along the curb.

She took Mr. Glen's arm and led him farther down the street from the burning building, so they were out of the way. She hadn't been in the house for long, but even that much exposure made her lungs feel like two pieces of sandpaper rubbing together with each breath.

"I don't like this," Cole muttered beside her. "It's almost as if the arsonist waited for Mr. Glen to leave before starting the place on fire."

"You think it's arson too?" She believed the same. "But if this is the shooter, what's the point of starting the place on fire?"

"Maybe he didn't realize you were gone," Cole pointed out. "He could have started the fire on the lower level to trap you upstairs."

She seethed with anger but tried not to show it. She was usually calm in a crisis. Even if she was the intended target, she needed to think logically about their next steps.

Earlier that morning, she'd called Rhy to let him know about the attempts against her and contacted the tow truck for her Jeep. Then she had started a list of perps she'd arrested over the past six months. The team's tech expert, Gabe Melrose, had agreed to begin vetting them through his various databases.

Now the perp had taken things to the next level. And the worst part was that Mr. Glen would suffer the most.

Wrestling back her temper, she turned to the older man. "Mr. Glen, we'll put you up in the closest hotel. You won't have to worry about anything, okay?" She eyed Cole who thankfully nodded in agreement. "We'll take care of paying for the room."

"No, no." Mr. Glen waved that away. "My daughter lives in Ravenswood. I can stay with her."

She remembered him mentioning a daughter but had never met the woman. "Are you sure? The repairs here could take a while." From what she remembered from her teammate Raelyn's fire, months at the very least.

"I'm sure." Mr. Glen shrugged. "She's been asking me to live with her for a while now. I guess this is a sign from God that it's time."

Despite her instinctive prayer, she wanted to scoff at the idea. Then again, things could be worse. She would never have forgiven herself if anything had happened to Mr. Glen. Maybe staying with his daughter was the right thing to do.

"We'll be glad to drop you off," Cole said. "We can leave here anytime."

"Yes. That would help." Mr. Glen turned from the fire, as if he couldn't bear to watch it a moment longer. His voice was low and gruff as he added, "Thank you."

She lifted her tortured gaze to Cole's. He offered a reassuring smile, but it didn't help her feel any better. This was obviously her fault. The perp who'd taken shots at her and chased her into a farm field had come here to set this fire. She didn't care if he'd waited until Mr. Glen was out of the building on his morning walk.

She wouldn't be satisfied until she'd tossed him behind bars, hopefully for the rest of his life. In her mind, this fire was attempted murder.

"Excuse me, are you the property owner?" A tall man with short blond hair crossed toward them. Recognizing arson investigator Mitch Callahan, she urged Mr. Glen forward. "Hey, Mitch. This is Mr. Glen Gleason. He is the property owner. I rent the upper-level flat from him."

"Mr. Gleason, I'm sorry for your loss," Mitch said, taking the older man's hand gently in his. "I'm arson investigator Mitch Callahan, and I'm here to figure out what happened."

"Someone torched it," Mr. Glen said curtly, getting some of his spunk back.

"Yes, I believe so." Mitch held the older man's gaze. "I suspect turpentine was used as the accelerant here. Do you keep turpentine around?"

"Yes, in the garage." Mr. Glen scowled. "You saying this guy used my stuff to set my house on fire?"

"It looks that way. Can you answer a few more questions for me?" Mitch asked. "Once that's done, the Red Cross can help find a place for you to stay." Mitch glanced at her. "For you, too, Jina."

"I'm fine." She wouldn't burden the Red Cross; they existed mostly on charitable donations. She made a decent living and would figure something out. "Mr. Glen has a daughter in Ravenswood he can stay with, but it wouldn't hurt for him to talk to the Red Cross too. Especially if he can't move back home for a long period of time."

"No need, I'll be fine with my daughter," Mr. Glen said firmly.

She curled her fingers into fists, imagining squaring off with the arsonist in the kickboxing ring. It would be extremely satisfying to plant her foot in his face.

Mitch asked Mr. Glen several questions, most of which he couldn't answer. When she explained about the shooting incident outside Mike's MMA gym, followed by the game of tag on the interstate, Mitch turned all his attention on her.

"Is there a police report on file?" Mitch asked, once she'd explained what had transpired.

"Yes, but the incidents took place in different jurisdictions." She grimaced. "The state patrol and Brookland."

"That's fine, I'll reach out to both entities." Mitch glanced between her and Cole. "Do you have any leads? Anyone in mind for the person behind this?"

"I sent a list of perps I arrested to my boss, Rhy Finnegan," she said. "It could be one of them, or it could be a man by the name of Rory Glick."

"Glick?" Mitch repeated as he jotted a note. "What's his deal?"

She sighed, wishing she didn't have to repeat the story. It wasn't one of her best moments. She never should have gone to the party with Rory in the first place. They'd had a few drinks, which had also been stupid. "He tried to rape me in college. I smashed a laptop against his head, called the police, and testified against him. He's on the sexual offender registry."

Mitch's expression turned sympathetic, which only made her mad. Maybe she'd made mistakes, but she'd also managed to fight back. Not just against Rory but firing at the hoodie stalker too. She wasn't helpless, and she resented anyone thinking she was.

"Wow, I'm surprised you didn't beat him to a pulp," Mitch said.

His comment almost made her smile. "I would be more than capable of that now, but the incident was a long time ago. Before I joined the police academy."

They discussed various possibilities for a few minutes before Mitch closed his notebook. "You've given me a great place to start. Please keep me in the loop if this guy makes another attempt against you."

"Sure." Rhy had given her the same instruction. The list of people that were becoming embroiled in this mess was growing longer by the second.

True to his word, Cole drove Mr. Glen to Ravenswood. Seeing how concerned his daughter Olivia was when she greeted her father made Jina feel a little better about the situation. Especially since Mr. Glen wasn't the target.

She was.

As they backed out of the driveway, she grabbed Cole's arm. "Hold on. We can't do this."

"Do what?" He looked confused.

"Interview Shelly." She tightened her grip. "We don't know who this guy is, and he might follow us out there. I refuse to put my pregnant sister and her husband in danger."

He sighed, then reluctantly nodded. "We'll talk to her over the phone, then."

She wanted to protest but forced a nod. The least she could do was to compromise on this. A phone call was far better than showing up on Shelly's doorstep.

And if she had her way, Shelly's husband, Greg, would

take her sister on an impromptu vacation until they had this perp behind bars.

———

AFTER SEEING the fire raging out of control, Cole understood Jina's concern about putting her sister in harm's way but doubted his boss would agree. Phone interviews were not nearly as good as talking to someone face-to-face.

A video call? It may help, but not by much.

This immediate threat to Jina overshadowed a ten-year-old cold case. He could tell himself the arson and gunshots targeting her wasn't his problem, but it didn't matter.

He was involved whether he liked it or not. Yes, the dead guy deserved justice but so did Jina.

And Mr. Glen.

Besides, for all he knew, the perp who'd smashed the dead man's skull could already be in prison. Or dead. It made more sense to focus on the more recent attempts against Jina.

"Okay, let's grab breakfast and regroup," he said. "Our breakfast sandwiches are cold and so is the coffee. I don't know about you, but I think more clearly on a full stomach."

"Yeah, I'm hungry too." She stared out the window for a moment. "Have you ever tried Rosie's Diner?"

"No, where is it?"

"Not far from here. Turn left at the next set of lights." She glanced at him. "You'll love it. Rosie makes the best pastries on the planet."

"Sounds good to me." He followed her directions until he was in front of a small restaurant with a half-full parking lot. "Does she serve breakfast this late? It's going on eleven."

"Yes, trust me." She flashed another rare smile. "Breakfast is her specialty."

"I'm game." He fought to keep his tone light, even though he felt himself sinking deeper under Jina's spell. Not that she had given him a single ounce of encouragement or acted remotely interested in him on a personal level.

No, this was on him. He needed to get this weird attraction to her under control. And quick.

Before he made a fool of himself. He could just imagine himself lying on his back on the gym floor, staring up at Jina's satisfied smirk at putting him there. Like every other guy before him. Irrationally, that image only made him want to kiss her.

Maybe he was losing his mind. Shaking his head he followed her inside the restaurant. The scent of apple and cinnamon perked him up.

"Jina, lass, it's wonderful to see you!" A round woman with a distinct Irish brogue and the brightest red hair he'd ever seen hustled over to greet them.

"Hi, Rosie. I was just telling Cole all about you."

"Ach, you flatter me." The redhead eyed him critically. "Aye, lad, Cole is it? That's a fine Irish name." She winked. "Any friend of Jina's is a friend of mine. I hope you're hungry. I have a fresh batch of apple turnovers hot from the oven."

"Apple turnovers?" His mouth watered. "I'd love one!"

Rosie let out a delighted laugh and gestured to an open booth. "Have a seat, then while I fetch the coffee and pastries."

He waited for Jina to choose a booth, then slid across from her. "I hope Rosie's cooking is as good as it smells."

"It's better." She waved a hand at the restaurant. "Usually it's packed, but we're here later than usual. Rosie's is a fan favorite of the tactical team." She frowned. "Now that I think about it, Rhy mentioned learning about the place from his brother Colin. Ironically, he's a firefighter, and I think Mitch is their cousin. I really hate that Mr. Glen might lose his duplex over this."

"Hey. Mr. Glen will be okay." He reached across the table to take her hand. "He seems pretty resilient."

"He wouldn't be in this predicament if not for me." She held his hand for a brief moment, then pulled away as Rosie returned with a coffeepot and two steaming apple turnovers.

Rosie set one in front of each of them then filled their cups. "There now, just let me know when you're ready to order."

"I'll have the full Irish," Jina said, before he'd had the chance to look at the menu.

"Ditto." He picked up his fork and tried the turnover. The pastry melted in his mouth. "Wow. This is the best turnover I've ever tasted."

"Told you." Jina took a bite too. "All of Rosie's baked goods are awesome, but her cinnamon rolls are the best."

"We'll have to come back to try them," he said, before realizing how that sounded. "I mean, now that you've shown me the restaurant, I'll be back."

"I'm sure your girlfriend will love it too." She sipped her coffee. "We should talk about the case. I understand you want to talk to Shelly in person, but I don't want to risk this guy finding her. We could try a halfway point, but only if I'm convinced it's safe."

He nodded. "First, I don't have a girlfriend. My wife, Renee, died of an aggressive form of leukemia three years ago. I'm not interested in dating. Second, I think we can start by doing a video call with your sister. Yes, I'd prefer to talk to her in person, but we'll start with the call to protect her. Third, I need that list of perps you put behind bars so we can narrow down our suspect pool."

She sat back in the seat, eyeing him thoughtfully. "You're rather methodical in your approach to investigations."

"Yep. And I get good results." Most of the time anyway. No detective solved every case that dropped on their desk. He hoped the cold case wouldn't be one of the unsolvable ones. "Any other questions?"

She shook her head. "I'm sorry to hear about your wife. That must have been difficult."

"It was. Renee was amazing." He stared down at his coffee for a moment. "We weren't that religious at the time, but when she died, she looked up at something in the distance and whispered about how beautiful it was before taking her last breath." He still got goose bumps when he remembered that moment. "I believe she's in a much better place."

"I, uh, that's interesting." She grimaced, then said, "We never went to church, and my dad didn't say anything like that when he died. He was angry about his heart attack and having to sell the farm. I often wonder . . ." She didn't finish.

"Faith is an interesting concept," he said after a long moment. "I understand that it's not easy to believe in God when you can't see Him or smell Him. But I will say that since I've started praying, I feel Him near me. That's what keeps my faith alive."

"Hard to imagine God would allow so many bad things to happen," she said with a shrug. "But I'm glad your faith works for you."

"It's difficult because the Devil walks among us," he

agreed. Then he decided to change the subject. "Tell me about those names. Any of them jump to the top of the list?"

"No. I'll send it to you once I have a new phone. Or access to a computer." She straightened. "I forgot; my laptop is in my overnight bag." She moved as if to stand, but he waved her off.

"Don't rush out now. We'll have time to look at the list in more detail when we're finished." At the rate these attacks were coming—three in a matter of hours—he wasn't letting her out of his sight anytime soon. "I was just curious if anyone specific jumped out at you. Someone who made it a point to threaten you."

"Most perps make threats." She sipped her coffee, then shrugged. "There was no one that stood out as being angry enough to come after me the moment they were released from jail. Especially if you consider this guy has shot at me, followed me in a car, and started a fire."

"Yeah, starting a fire is not common for most perps seeking revenge." He stopped from saying more as Rosie delivered their meals. The full Irish was more food than he'd expected, but it looked incredible. "Thanks, Rosie."

"Enjoy." Rosie scurried off to her next customer.

Jina looked at him expectantly. He rubbed his face, wondering if he had apple turnover crumbs on his lips. "What?"

"I figured you were going to pray." She folded her hands in her lap. "Many of my teammates are believers, so I usually hold back scarfing my food until they've said grace."

"Ah, well, sure." He didn't usually pray before meals, but since she'd mentioned it, he figured this was a good time to thank God for keeping them safe. "Lord Jesus, we are grateful for this wonderful food we are about to eat. We thank You for keeping Mr. Glen and both of us safe in Your care. Amen."

Jina gave a curt nod but didn't echo the prayer. Instead, she dug into her meal with gusto. After witnessing the vigor in which she worked out at the MMA gym, he wasn't surprised she could put a meal away like an offensive lineman.

They ate in silence, enjoying the meal. He understood why Jina had suggested the place. He'd never had a full Irish breakfast and knew he'd have to return at some point to try the rest of Rosie's menu. Especially her baked goods.

When Rosie brought the bill, he quickly grabbed it. Jina scowled, but he shook his head. "My treat. You're only here because I need to talk to your sister."

"Yeah, well, that move may have saved my life," she said somberly.

He gave Rosie his credit card. She returned a few minutes later, beaming at them. "Ach, don't be a stranger now, Cole. You either, lass. I hope you'll come back very soon."

"I promise," he said with a smile. "Best meal ever."

"Ach, flattery will get you two coffees to go if you'd like," Rosie said with a laugh.

She hurried off to fill a couple of to-go cups. He eyed Jina as they waited. "I don't want you to be upset or think I'm trying anything funny, but we should head to my place to call Shelly." As her gaze narrowed, he sighed. "If you'd prefer to head to the Peabody Police Department, that's fine too. It's not as private as I'd like. Not that I believe your sister will reveal any big dark secrets," he hastily added.

She waited until Rosie brought their cups, then rose to her feet. "Okay, we'll head to your place. For now."

"Great." He was glad she trusted him at least this much.

It burned to know two different men had betrayed her—one stalker and the other attempting to sexually assault her.

Hard to blame her for being cautious.

Once they were settled in the SUV, he drove toward Peabody. She rummaged in the overnight bag, pulling out a laptop.

"Do you mind if I use your phone as a hot spot?" she asked, booting it up.

"Ah, sure." He made the hot spot available to her. "Can I give you my email address?"

"Yes." She typed as he spoke. "Email sent."

Before he could respond, his phone rang. She quickly ended the hot spot connection so he could answer it. Seeing the ME's number on the screen, he considered sending the call to voice mail. Then he decided to accept the call. "This is Detective Roberts."

"Dr. Swain from the ME's office. You asked for an update, so I thought I'd call."

"Were you able to match our vic's dental records?"

"Not yet, I'm waiting for them to come in. But I did find some clothing remnants that might be of interest."

"Clothing remnants?" He glanced at Jina. "I figured there was nothing left after all this time. Most clothing decomposes within five years."

"That's true, but in this particular case, the perp was wearing a synthetic fleece, which can take a very long time to decompose. Especially since it appears a wool blanket was wrapped around the body. There were some woolen threads that were found with the bits of fleece."

His stomach knotted as the realization hit. "Fleece, as in a sweatshirt?"

"Yes, that's correct. A black hoodie sweatshirt to be exact. We have the eyelets from the string that went around the hood and several patches of black fleece that had not decomposed yet."

A black hoodie sweatshirt. Just like the one Jina's stalker had worn.

A cold chill washed over him. Was he wrong about her?

Jina was a tough cop, able to hold her own even in the face of a personal attack. It wasn't a stretch to imagine her slamming a bat or some other blunt object into the stalker's head to kill him, then hiding his body on the outskirts of the farm where she believed no one would ever find him.

Until now.

CHAPTER FIVE

It was bad enough to learn the dead man on her farm had been wearing a black fleece hoodie, but the flash of suspicion in Cole's eyes stabbed deep. How could he think she had killed that guy, hid the body, and then went on to become a cop?

Granted, she'd put several guys down on the mat at the gym. But that was a long way from killing them. She hadn't even killed Rory, despite his attempt to rape her.

"Let me know when you get a positive dental ID," Cole said.

"Will do." The ME ended the call, leaving a long, strained silence stretching between them.

"I didn't kill him." The words popped out before she could take them back. She didn't appreciate having to defend herself.

"Maybe you didn't mean to kill him," he said. "You admitted to wounding him by shooting your father's gun. Then you followed his blood trail. He could have fallen over a tree root and bashed his head against a rock. He died, so you panicked and buried him."

"That is not what happened." Yet she could easily hear some prosecutor pressing this theory of the case in front of a judge. And what proof did she have that she hadn't killed anyone? Especially after she'd slammed the laptop into Rory's head. As if that act of self-preservation wouldn't come back to bite her in the butt. "Believe what you want, but I did not kill him."

Neither of them spoke for several minutes. When Cole pulled into the driveway of a small green-sided ranch house, she decided that going inside would be a bad idea. In a swift movement, she pushed open her door, grabbed her bag, and got out of the car. Without looking at Cole, she turned and walked down the driveway to the street.

Not having a phone meant she couldn't call for a rideshare. But she could walk to the nearest business to borrow a phone. She hadn't wanted to go to Madison to see Shelly for fear of the bad guy following her, but maybe she could see her sister if she took a method of travel that would be difficult to track.

Like a bus.

Too bad she had no idea where the closest bus station was located. Would she have to go all the way back down to Milwaukee to catch a bus ride to Madison? Probably.

"Jina, wait."

She shook her head and kept walking. Then she abruptly stopped as she remembered his intent to interview her sister. What was she doing? She needed to wait until that task was done before heading out.

She reluctantly turned to face him, hating that she'd reacted rashly. "I'll stay while you chat with Shelly. After that, I'm out."

"Obviously, you can do what you want," Cole said. "But

considering the danger, it would be better for us to work together on finding the shooter turned arsonist."

"Why bother since you're already trying to figure out how to arrest me for murder? Or aggravated assault. Manslaughter. Maybe assault with a deadly weapon." She knew there were several different charges that he could recommend the DA press against her. "Any of those charges would result in me serving jail time, not to mention ruining my career."

"I haven't arrested you for anything," he pointed out.

"But you're thinking about it." She held his gaze, and to his credit, he didn't deny it. "I didn't kill him, accidentally or on purpose. And I absolutely did not hide his body on my parents' land."

"Maybe you and Shelly can help me figure out who did."

She tightened her grip on her overnight bag, resisting the urge to throw it at him. Despite her strenuous workouts in the MMA gym, she wasn't prone to violence. Giving in to a stupid childish impulse now would only make things worse.

A good fighter always remained in control.

Taking a deep calming breath, she closed the distance between them. "We can talk to Shelly. Just be prepared to be disappointed."

He nodded and led the way up to the small ranch house. He unlocked the door, pushed it open, then stepped back so she could enter first.

The interior was clean and comfortable. She had to give him points for not being a total slob like her teammate Flynn. She headed into the kitchen where Cole's laptop was sitting on the table, an empty coffee cup beside it.

Apparently, he'd been working this morning, much like she had been.

Before the fire that had damaged Mr. Glen's two-story home.

Her anger and frustration with Cole thinking the worst of her faded. Finding this guy who'd hurt Mr. Glen was her top priority.

Clearing her name was secondary. Not that she planned to accept her fate without fighting back. It abruptly occurred to her that she needed to fill Rhy and Joe in as soon as possible.

It wouldn't help to wait until her position on the tactical team was compromised. She preferred owning up to her mistakes.

And being honest with Cole about the stalker she'd shot twelve years ago had been one doozy of a mistake. If she'd just kept her mouth shut, he wouldn't be looking at her with suspicion.

So much for innocent until proven guilty. Oh, she knew most cops approached their investigations from the opposite viewpoint, presumed guilty until cleared. She usually did too. But that didn't sit well now that she was the suspect in question.

"Would you like more coffee?" Cole asked, interrupting her thoughts.

"Sure." She dropped her overnight bag on the floor, then sank into a chair, watching as he made a fresh pot. He moved with a lithe grace, comfortable in his own skin. Maybe because he wasn't trying to impress her. Quite the opposite. She sensed he still loved his dead wife, Renee.

He looked good in a sports coat. Too bad he was the enemy.

"Does your sister work?" he asked, returning to the

table. "I only ask because I don't know if we'll catch her at home or at her job."

"Shelly works from home; she's a medical record coder." Jina knew that Shelly hoped to work part time after the baby was born since her husband was a physical therapist. "If she's busy, you'll have to leave a message. But I'm sure she'll call back as soon as she can."

"Sounds like a plan." He took out his phone and then glanced at a small notebook. It was disconcerting to see her name, number, and address written there along with Shelly's name, address, and phone number.

No surprise, his call went to Shelly's voice mail. After leaving a message, he glanced at her. "Do you want to start going through the list of names?"

"Yes, but I need to call my boss." She gestured to his phone. "Do you mind if I borrow that for a minute?"

"Sure." He handed it over. She rose and walked into the living room for some privacy to make the call. Thankfully, Rhy answered on the first ring.

"Captain Finnegan."

"Rhy, it's Jina. I wanted to let you know that I don't have my phone. I'm borrowing one from—a friend." She cleared her throat. "I appreciate you giving me time off work. The shooter who came after me last night showed up this morning and set fire to Mr. Glen Gleason's duplex. I already spoke to Mitch Callahan but thought you and Joe should know too."

"Anyone hurt?" Rhy asked.

"We're fine. We drove Mr. Glen to his daughter's home in Ravenswood. I, uh, will figure out someplace to stay. Did Gabe Melrose have time to dig into the list of names I sent?"

"He's just started. I promise he'll call if he finds something. Do you want me to let Cassidy know? You can probably bunk with her for a few days."

"I'll check in with Cass later." Jina didn't want to impose on her fellow teammate. Now that Raelyn was married to Pastor Isaiah Washington, she and Cassidy had grown a bit closer. But that didn't mean Cassidy wanted Jina to live with her indefinitely. Besides, Jina preferred having her own space.

"Keep us in the loop," Rhy said. "The team is here for you if you need anything. I don't like knowing one of my cops is in harm's way."

"Thanks." She was touched by his offer. Maybe she was being stubbornly independent, but she wasn't ready to call for reinforcements. "I'll let you know."

"Take care," Rhy said.

"I will. Thanks." She ended the call, thinking about Rhy's suggestion to contact Cassidy, when the phone in her hand rang. Recognizing Shelly's number, she quickly answered, walking back to the kitchen. "Hi, Shelly, it's Jina. I'm here with Detective Roberts."

"Hey, Jina, what is this about?" Shelly asked. "I was shocked to hear this guy wants to talk to me."

"I know, but here, I'll let him fill you in." She handed the phone to Cole.

"Ms. Strom? This is Detective Cole Roberts. If you don't mind, I'd like to use a video call."

Jina assumed her sister agreed because Cole ended the call, then started over using the video call app. Moments later, she could see her sister's face on the small screen. Jina stood over Cole's shoulder so she could watch the interaction.

"I don't understand. What is this about?" Shelly asked, her brow furrowed.

"I have a few routine questions for you," Cole said. "You lived on your parents' farm until you were a sophomore in high school, is that correct?"

"Yes. We moved after my dad had a heart attack."

"Do you remember anything strange happening back then?"

Shelly glanced at Jina before answering. She gave her sister a subtle nod, indicating she could go ahead and tell him. The cat was out of the bag now anyway. "Yes, Jina had some trouble with a stalker. He climbed into her bedroom window late on a Saturday night. Jina used our dad's handgun to scare him off."

"Did you see Jina shoot him?" Cole asked.

"No, but I heard the gunshot. Then we ran outside to see if we could find him. Jina found some blood on the window and the ground. We followed it, but then it disappeared." Shelly looked concerned. "Has that guy come back to make trouble for Jina? She was only trying to protect us. He had no right to come into our house, especially her bedroom!"

"No, he hasn't come back to make trouble for anyone," Cole assured her. "I'm going to text you a photograph. I'd like you to tell me if you recognize the man in the picture."

"Okay." Shelly frowned. Then her face disappeared while Cole texted the picture of Bradley Crow. After a long moment, Shelly nodded. "Yeah, he looks familiar."

What? Jina leaned closer. "Where did you see him?"

Another pause as Shelly considered that. "I think he was at the custard stand when I went there to see you." Her sister tipped her head to the side. "You don't remember?"

"No. I didn't recognize him." She was stunned by Shelly's admission. "You're sure you saw him?"

"I think so. But it was a long time ago. I could be

wrong." Her sister looked uncertain. "I mean, I'm not sure I'd want to swear to it in court. Why? Who is he?"

Cole glanced over his shoulder at her, before turning back to Shelly. "His name is Bradley Crow. He was reported missing twelve years ago. You saw him outside the custard stand where Jina worked? Can you describe what he was wearing?"

"I think so, yes." Shelly looked nervous now. "He had a dark sweatshirt on, with the hood up."

Jina's stomach clenched at that. Was it possible Crow was her stalker? And the dead guy buried on the farm? If so, how in the world had he gotten there?

"What made you remember him?" Cole asked. "He must have stuck out in your mind for a reason."

"I only noticed because he watched Jina while she worked, like with a single-minded focus. It was a little creepy." Shelly flushed, then added, "But I was only fifteen at the time, so I could be wrong. I wouldn't feel comfortable testifying in court that they were one and the same."

"I understand," Cole said with a smile. "Thanks for your cooperation. That's all I have for now, but I may need to talk to you again in the future."

"Jina? Are you okay?" Shelly asked, clearly worried about what she'd revealed.

"I'm fine, don't worry about me. Just take care of yourself and that baby, okay?" She forced a smile for her sister's sake. "We'll talk later."

"Okay, sounds good. Bye." Shelly ended the video call.

"I had no idea she saw him at the custard stand," Jina said, after a pause. "Doesn't mean he's my stalker. A lot of kids wore hoodies back then." She was getting tired of defending herself. She snagged her bag from the floor and headed for the door.

"Hold on. I thought you wanted to help investigate the shooter?" Cole asked.

She hesitated, turning to look at him. He wasn't looking at her with suspicion, but it was only a matter of time before he had a positive ID on the dead guy.

Sticking around to work the shooter/arsonist case with him wasn't smart. Yet at the same time, she needed to find the man who'd set fire to Mr. Glen's home. Stay or go? It was shocking how much she wanted to stay.

"Fine." She dropped her bag near the door and crossed to the counter to get some coffee. She'd likely regret this later, but for now, she could use Cole's help. Besides, wasn't there some saying that advised keeping your friends close but your enemies closer?

Maybe sticking with Cole would help her in the long run. At least that way she'd be prepared prior to his arresting her.

———

COLE DIDN'T WANT to believe Jina had anything to do with Bradley Crow's death. Yet he wasn't exactly impartial either. He liked her. Admired her. And yes, he was attracted to her.

So why on earth was he encouraging her to stick around to work the case? Because he was a glutton for punishment, that's why. The DA's office would go nuts if they found out he'd had Jina with him while interviewing her sister. And worse, that he'd worked with Jina on another case prior to her being arrested.

"I was thinking we should dig into Rory Glick's whereabouts for the time frame in question," Jina said, carrying two cups of coffee to the table. He was surprised

when she handed him one. "My thought was to find businesses near Mike's gym that may have camera footage.
Maybe we can pick him out as being nearby at the time of
the shooting."

He nodded thoughtfully. "That's a good angle to
pursue."

Jina flushed, then gestured at the computer. "The only
problem is that I have not seen Rory in years. It would be
nice if we could get an updated photo of him."

"The sexual offender registry updates a perp's picture
every ten years." He took control of the keyboard to bring
Rory Glick's picture up. He grimaced. "Unfortunately, it
doesn't appear his is one of them."

She peered at the screen. "You're right. According to
the information listed there, he's twenty-two in this photo. I
guess this was taken after he was released."

He committed Glick's facial features to memory.
"Hopefully, he hasn't changed that much. Give me a
minute to call Mike. See if he knows where the closest
cameras might be located."

She nodded, sipping her coffee as he made the call.
Mike answered right away. "Cole, do you have any more
information about what happened last night?"

"Unfortunately, I don't." He didn't think filling him in
on the arson was smart. They didn't know for sure the perp
was the shooter. "I'm calling because we need to figure out a
way to find this guy. I don't believe the strip mall has
cameras. Do you know of any other businesses nearby that
might have them?"

"There's a gas station two miles west of the gym that has
security cameras." There was a brief pause, before Mike
said, "I don't know of any others offhand. The one here in
the gym is only pointed at the front door so that I know

when people are coming in. I can check it but doubt the image captured anyone lurking around outside."

"Please do check your camera," he said.

"Are you sure about the strip mall?" Mike asked. "There could be a camera back there."

"They didn't seem to be cash-heavy establishments," he said, remembering the brief glimpse he got of the place. "But we'll double-check."

"Is Jina okay?" Mike asked.

"Yeah, she's fine." Mike was a former cop; he'd injured his shooting hand during a scuffle with a perp. And he was also single. His interest in Jina put Cole's teeth on edge. Not that he had any claims on her. Quite the opposite. She was off-limits by a mile. "I'll keep you updated if we learn anything more."

"Sounds good. Call if you need help," Mike said. "Tell Jina I'm glad she's okay."

"I will. Thanks, Mike." He ended the call, glancing at her. "Mike's glad you're not hurt."

She frowned. "He should know as well as anyone I can take care of myself."

Her puzzled response, seemingly not realizing Mike's interest was personal, shouldn't have made him smile. "He mentioned a gas station. That should be our first stop."

"Okay." She took another sip of her coffee, then set it aside. "I'm ready to hit the road."

"Hang on." He used the computer to access a map app to look up the strip mall. She leaned over to see the screen.

"We should have considered cameras last night," she said with disgust.

"Yeah, well technically, it's not our case." He flashed a smile. "But that won't stop us from looking into it."

"I like how you think." Her tone was light, but her

expression turned somber. He wanted to reassure her that he wasn't viewing her as a key suspect.

But he couldn't. Because the time would come when he might have no choice.

"I don't see any cameras, do you?" He had zoomed in on the map app to get a three-dimensional image of the strip mall.

"No, but this software may not be up to date." She leaned back. "We'll have to swing by to double-check anyway."

She seemed anxious to go. He closed the laptop, then headed back outside.

He was surprised she'd grabbed her overnight bag. Seeing it made him wonder about the damage to her upper-level apartment. Smoke and water damage for sure, but had the fire gotten that far? Would there be anything left to salvage?

"Do you want to stop along the way to pick up a phone?" he asked, opening the car door for her.

"Yeah, that would be great." She tossed her bag into the back seat. "But let's check the cameras first. I'm worried they may not keep the video for very long."

"Okay." He quickly slid in behind the wheel and headed out. The MMA gym was in Brookland but close to Peabody. As he drove, he looked for other possible locations where they might find security cameras. There were dozens of them along the main roads, but Mike's MMA gym was a good mile or two from the well-traveled area.

He headed straight for the gas station, which also housed a small convenience store. He parked along the side of the building, then accompanied Jina inside. He took the lead, showing his badge and identifying himself as a detective, without specifying his jurisdiction was limited to the Peabody Police Department.

"I'd like to see your video camera footage for the past twenty-four hours," he said.

"Is this about that shooting at the gym?" The clerk's eyes bulged with interest. "I heard the guy got away."

"Yes, has someone else already come to look at the video?"

"Not yet. But I saved it just in case." The clerk held up his hand while he handled a pump request, then added, "The boss said we're supposed to cooperate with the investigation."

"Great. Let's see it."

The clerk led them back to a door marked employees only. There was a small office where Cole assumed the store manager worked. The kid went around to bring up the video on the computer, then stepped back. "Sorry, I have to go back out front. I'm here alone."

"Thanks, we can manage from here." He took a seat behind the desk, while Jina hovered nearby.

He started the video, increasing the speed so they could see what was happening without spending the entire day there. Unfortunately, the gas station was busy, so it took more time than he would have liked to slow the video for each dark SUV that came into view.

Police work was slow and tedious in general, but watching endless video with Jina hovering over his shoulder was agonizing. He tried not to be distracted by her nearness, focusing instead on trying to spot the SUV without plates with a driver that looked like Rory Glick.

There were several times of the day that no cars came into the station, but after two hours, he stopped the video and rubbed his eyes. "Maybe we should send a copy to my computer. At this rate, we'll be here all day."

"Let's keep going a little while longer," she said. "I'm sure he came by during the day before heading back at night."

"Okay." He resumed the video, slowing the speed when another dark SUV came into view. The Wisconsin rule about front license plates had changed; they were no longer required. Yet most of the cars he saw had them. Like this one.

Forty-five minutes later, Jina said, "There. Do you see it? That car doesn't have a rear plate."

He had missed it, so he backed up the video. She was right. A black Honda SUV without a rear plate sat next to the gas pump on the farthest side of the station. It was possible that there were two black Honda SUVs without license plates, but not likely. He zoomed in, but the image was blurry. And the pump itself blocked the view of the driver.

"Let's send this to Gabe," Jina said with excitement in her voice. When she noticed his confused look, she added, "He's our tactical team tech expert. He'll be able to clean this up to get a better view of the driver."

"Okay. Let me see if I can copy a good section of video." He might not be Gabe the tech expert, but he knew his way around computers. He was able to copy the video, sending it to his email address. When he finished, he stood. "You were right, he did come by in the daytime to scope things out."

"Yeah, I just wish we could see his face." Jina stretched her back. "I hope Gabe can work his magic. I'm convinced this guy has a prison record. We just need a good enough photo to use in the police database."

"I agree." He headed back out to the gas station. "Do you want anything before we go?"

"Nope. I'm good. Let's head back to the strip mall." She looked eager to get to work.

He couldn't help but think Jina would make a good detective. His partner, Kevin Hunt, was out on paternity leave, his wife having recently delivered a baby boy. Kevin was a good cop, but Cole had secretly enjoyed working alone the past few days.

Back outside, they rounded the corner of the gas station. Thinking about the strip mall, and the possible clues they might find, it took a minute for him to notice the guy slinking behind the building.

"Look out!" His shout was cut off by the sound of gunfire. Pulling his weapon, he dropped to a knee and glanced toward Jina.

His heart about stopped in his chest when he didn't see her.

"Jina! Are you hit?" Praying she wasn't, he moved along the length of the SUV hoping to get a line on the gunman.

Then he heard a car engine roar to life. He bolted from his vehicle and ran toward the back of the gas station in time to see a black Honda with no license plate peeling away.

CHAPTER SIX

That had been too close. Jina had been in more dangerous situations than she could count since joining Rhy's tactical team, but this was the first time she'd heard the whistle of a bullet and felt the rush of air as it went past her ear. She lifted her hand to her temple to check for blood.

Thankfully, she hadn't been hit.

A flash of anger hit hard. Who was this guy? She was tired of being used as target practice. While his first attempts to hit her had gone high and wide, this one had not. Either the first attempt had been a scare tactic, or he'd honed his shooting skills since last night. Before she could move along the side of Cole's SUV, he rounded the front end. Seeing her, he visibly relaxed. "Are you okay?"

"Yes. Was that his car I heard?" She had been slow to react, which wasn't like her. She rose from her crouch and walked toward him. "We should have anticipated he'd come back."

"I know." Cole's expression turned grim. "I didn't think he'd take the risk in the bright light of day. The way he showed up here as if realizing we'd be trying to find him makes me wonder if he has law enforcement background."

That possibility hadn't occurred to her. "A cop would likely hit his target. And I also think a cop would have been smart enough not to stop for gas so close to the gym."

"Maybe he's an academy dropout or was injured on the job in some way." He shrugged. "Could be his skills are rusty."

"I don't know why a former cop would try to kill me." Maybe she didn't make friends as easily as her female counterparts, but she wasn't a bad person. There had been some fellow cops who'd spread rumors about her being cold and frigid because she hadn't wanted to date them, but that shouldn't cause something like this.

Even the guys she'd challenged to spar at Mike's hadn't been physically hurt. Their pride may have taken a beating, but so what? In her humble opinion, they'd deserved it. One of the guys, Jimmy, had point-blank asked if she'd joined the gym to find a man. As if she couldn't possibly be there for a strenuous workout or to hone her fighting skills.

"We should probably talk to Mike again." She spoke loud enough to be heard over the screech of sirens. The local cops would not be thrilled to know she and Cole had been involved in yet another shooting incident. "I don't want to believe any of the members are involved, but it might be nice to know if any of those guys I put down are former cops or military."

"Sounds good." He turned to head to the back of the gas station. "Let's search for shell casings. It would be good to match them with the ones found at the gym last night."

She joined him along the back of the building. Bits of garbage littered the ground not far from the dumpster located back there. The stench was bad, but she'd experienced worse. There was no need to use flashlights, and it only took a moment to find the glint of sun bouncing off the brass.

"It looks like the same caliper." She didn't touch the casing, knowing the police would want to see where it was. "Can you get a picture with your phone?"

"Sure." Cole did as she asked. "There has to be one more. I believe he shot twice."

They split up to cover more ground. She didn't see anything in her search area, but Cole waved her over. "Found it. He stood close to the dumpster to fire this round."

She went over to see for herself, then turned to review the line of sight. It was sobering to realize how close he'd been. In fact, she wasn't sure how he'd missed from this distance.

"God was watching over you," Cole said as if reading her thoughts. It was exactly what Rhy, Joe, or the other guys would have said. She wasn't sure how to respond, mostly because she was starting to wonder if he was right about that.

Then she silently chided herself for being foolish.

Two squads pulled up near Cole's SUV. Suppressing a sigh, she headed back over to give her statement. She had not been on the victim end of things since college and found it really annoying to be in that position now.

Was that this guy's intent? Shooting and starting fires just to force her into feeling like a victim?

"I'm Peabody Detective Cole Roberts, and this MPD Officer Jina Wheeler." Cole flashed his gold shield, so she pulled her badge out too. Better to show their creds since they were both carrying. "An unknown perp fired at us from behind the gas station. Two shots and we can show you where both shell casings are located."

"Roberts and Wheeler?" The officer with the last name Howard scowled. "Were you involved in a shooting last night too?"

"That's correct. Likely the same perp." Jina gestured for Officers Howard and Tyson to follow her to the back of the gas station. "We're hoping you can match these shell casings to the ones found last night outside Mike's MMA gym."

"We'll do that. Did you get a look at him?" Tyson asked.

"No, I didn't." She glanced at Cole who also shook his head. "He came closer to hitting me this time. Missed by a fraction of an inch."

Cole scowled as the two officers exchanged looks. "Sorry to hear that," Officer Howard said. "Our Detective Irving tried to reach out to you."

She flushed. "Yeah, sorry. I left my phone in the apartment and couldn't get back in to grab it because of the fire."

"Fire?" Tyson echoed. "What happened?"

"We have reason to believe the fire was set by the same person who was just here firing at Jina," Cole said. "Arson Investigator Mitch Callahan is working the case."

"Two shootings and a fire?" Howard frowned. "Perps don't often change their MO midstream."

"Yeah, well, this guy seems determined to get my attention." And he had, she silently added. The escalating attacks were forcing her to play defense.

"What about the vehicle?" Tyson asked.

"We have reason to believe he's driving a black Honda SUV without license plates," Cole said. When he didn't elaborate on the video footage of that same vehicle they'd gotten from the gas station, she kept her mouth shut too.

It was likely Cole was waiting to share that information with Detective Irving. At this point, she figured it was better to let Cole take the lead.

Besides, Irving wasn't going to be the one to solve this thing. No, it was clear that she and Cole working together had the advantage when it came to finding this guy. For one thing, she was the target.

A plan of setting herself as bait was already forming in the back of her mind. Drastic and risky? Yes. She had every intention of being the fun auntie to her sister's baby. She'd prefer to get some answers on the few leads they had in the works prior to going that route, but if they didn't pan out?

They'd have no choice but to implement plan B.

She and Cole answered more questions before they were free to leave. But just then another car pulled up, and she heard Cole groan under his breath.

"Detective Irving?" she asked in a low voice.

"I assume so." Cole put his arm around her waist in a gesture that normally would have gotten him flipped onto his back. Yet somehow, she didn't mind as they approached the two detectives emerging from a dark-blue sedan.

"Are you Detective Cole Roberts?" The female detective looked pointedly at Cole.

"Yes. And this is Officer Wheeler." Cole stepped forward to shake hands with both cops. She followed suit.

"I'm Detective Irving, and this is my partner, Detective Klem." Irving was the female detective and appeared to be taking the lead. "We heard about the shooting last night and tried to reach out to Officer Wheeler this morning." Detective Irving's tone sounded accusatory. "I left two messages."

"Don't have my phone," she said. "Sorry."

"We'd like you to come with us to the Brookland PD,"

Detective Klem said, his approach far more laid back. "We have several questions that we'd like to go over with you."

Jina swallowed a groan, but of course, Cole nodded. "Fine, we can meet you there."

"We'd rather you drove with us," Irving said, her eyes narrowing.

"No." Cole's blunt refusal made her smile, but she coughed to hide it. "I'm not leaving my SUV here. And Jina is a victim, not a perp. We'll drive on our own."

The two Brookland detectives exchanged a long look, then Klem nodded. "Sure, we understand."

Detective Irving scowled but turned to jump back into the car. Jina couldn't help but wonder why the female detective had an attitude. It wasn't as if she'd asked for some idiot to shoot at her. She glanced at Cole who was frowning at the two detectives who were waiting for them to get into the SUV.

"I hope this doesn't take long," she muttered, wrenching the passenger-side door open.

"I agree." Cole started the engine and pulled out behind the sedan. "Do you get that a lot?"

"Get what?" She didn't understand until he gestured to the sedan in front of them. "Oh, you mean Irving's attitude? Not really. Usually, cops are decent to each other. I'm not sure who put a bug up her butt."

"Jealousy," Cole said. "She knows you're a beautiful, smart, capable police officer." He grinned. "And she hasn't even seen you in action at the gym."

His compliment shouldn't have made her blush. She willed herself not to react. "I'm just trying to do a job, the same as she is."

"Yeah, I know."

"How come you don't have a partner?" She had

wondered about that last night when he'd mentioned coming to the gym to interview her. "Like those two, I thought all detectives worked in pairs."

"My partner is out on paternity leave, so I'm working solo for a few weeks."

"Oh, I see." That may be why Cole was given the cold case that he'd had very little time to work on. She squelched a flash of guilt, reminding herself she hadn't asked for this.

He glanced at his watch. "I'll call Mike when we're finished. I'm sure he'll meet us at my place without a problem."

"Your place?" She frowned. "Why would you ask him to come there? We can talk to him on the phone. Besides, we still have to check out the strip mall, remember?"

"Not happening, this perp could be waiting for us there."

"Yes, all the more reason to head over as soon as possible." She tried not to sound annoyed. "Besides, we won't be caught off guard by his being there this time. Frankly, I'm anxious to meet with this guy, up close and personal."

His jaw tightened, and he didn't answer. She could tell he wasn't happy but that didn't matter.

She sat back in her seat, determined to keep moving forward with the case. They needed to find this jerk before he could hurt anyone else.

THE MEETING at the Brookland PD took far longer than it should have. Cole was losing his patience fast, especially with Detective Irving's snotty attitude toward Jina.

"We're done here." He abruptly stood when Irving asked the same question she'd started with over an hour ago. "You have my contact information if something changes."

"You're not done until I say so," Irving protested.

"How about you go out and do some real detective work?" Cole stared the woman down. "You might want to start by going back to that gas station to review the video."

That caught Irving and Klem off guard, giving him a spurt of satisfaction.

"Yes, you'll find the black Honda SUV without plates was there about seven o'clock last evening," Jina said, rising to her feet. "The pump blocked the perp, though, so there's no clear image of his face. But you should probably take a look at it for yourself."

"You already got the video?" Irving demanded, as if someone had stolen all her candy.

Cole glanced at Klem who appeared embarrassed. "You need to be out there doing your own legwork. Sitting around and waiting for a victim to return a call isn't how cases get solved." He stepped toward the door with Jina at his side. "We'll keep you in the loop if we find anything pertinent to the case."

"You can't work this case," Irving sputtered. "We have jurisdiction here."

Cole ignored her. He opened the door for Jina and followed her out of the interview without another word. Neither of them said anything until they were back outside in the SUV.

"That was fun," Jina drawled sarcastically. "Irving seems to think I'm being targeted on purpose just to ruin her day."

"She's something," he agreed. He wasn't impressed with Irving at all, but Klem seemed reasonable. "Hopefully,

Klem will keep her on track. I have a feeling we'll be hearing from them again very soon."

"Oh goody." She gestured to the big box store up ahead. "That reminds me, I need a replacement phone. Let's stop now since we're here. I want to be sure Shelly can reach me in an emergency."

"Fine with me." He was glad for the reprieve since he did not want to head over to Mike's as planned. Sure, they could approach the place with caution, but there were several locations where their perp could be hiding.

While Jina spoke to the store rep about her phone, he used his to call Mike.

"What's up, Cole?" Mike asked.

"I know we've already discussed the guys at the gym not being the shooter, but things have changed. We need to know if any of those guys are involved in law enforcement or the military."

There was a long silence as Mike considered that. "I can put together a list of names of those I know, but that won't cover them all."

"I understand. Are you at the gym now?" He was surprised to see that Jina had already picked out a phone and was heading over to the checkout line. Apparently, she was a no-nonsense shopper. "Jina wants to head over, but I'm worried our guy is hanging out nearby."

"Why would he?" Mike asked.

Cole filled him in on the gas station shooting.

Mike whistled. "Not good. I can see why you're thinking cop or military. I'll go through my files and my memory. I'll come up with a few names for you."

"Thanks, that would be great." He headed over to join Jina. "We don't want to think the worst of your gym members either, but someone is gunning for her, and I want to cover all bases."

"Understood. I'll let you know if I hear anything suspicious."

"Thanks. Later." He ended the call as Jina eyed him warily. "That was Mike. He's going to make a list of the guys with law enforcement or military background." He gestured to her phone. "We should head to my place so you can power it up and get your contacts uploaded."

She looked as if she might argue but then nodded. "Fine. Once that's done, we'll talk about next steps."

He followed her to the SUV, feeling certain he wouldn't like her idea of what they should work on next. Once they were back at his place, Jina went to work on her phone, while he opened his laptop to find the video he'd sent to his email address.

Reviewing the grainy video again, he slowed it to look frame by frame, attempting to get a better look at their perp. He froze the screen at one point, trying to decide if the guy had dark hair or had a dark ball cap on his head.

"Do you mind if I use your phone to call Gabe?" Jina came over to sit beside him. "I sent him the video but haven't had time to follow up."

"Sure." He unlocked his screen and handed her the phone. "Put the call on speaker."

"Okay." She made the call, setting the phone on the table. "Hi, Gabe, it's Jina and Detective Cole Roberts from the Peabody PD."

"Hey, Jina, I got this video you sent," Gabe said. "I'm afraid there isn't much I can do with it, though. I cleaned it up, but the guy is standing behind the pump, almost as if he knew where the cameras were located."

"Yeah, that's our theory too," Jina admitted.

"Gabe, this is Cole. Do you think his hair is dark brown or black, or is he wearing a hat?"

"Good question. Hang on." He heard typing in the background. "Okay, I'll send this cleaned-up version back to you so you can judge for yourself. I think he's wearing a hat; there's a bit of a line along the side of his head. He might have dark hair beneath the hat, but again, it's hard to tell."

"Thanks, I'll take a look." He hadn't noticed the line Gabe mentioned. "I'm not sure the hair color matters; he could have dyed it to make himself look different."

"Hair dye works best to make light hair darker, not the other way around," Jina said. "Hey, Gabe, did you get anything on doing the look back on the perps I've arrested in the past few years?"

"I have two names for you," Gabe said. "Carson Rinko and Jorge Navarro. Both guys have been released in the past year. Rinko was released in November of last year and Navarro in February of this year."

He made a note of both names as Jina frowned. "I'd have expected the perp to have been released much sooner than that," she said with a sigh.

"There's one guy coming up for parole next month," Gabe said. "His name is Terry Straub."

"If he's still in prison, he's not our guy," Jina said.

"Is his real name Terrance?" Cole asked, eyeing Jina. "Could be Terrance has a brother or close friend doing his dirty work."

"If we're going to add friends and relatives of these perps, we'll never narrow the list down," she protested.

He understood her frustration. "We'll only look at Terrance Straub's friends and family. Maybe they're worried you'll show up at the parole hearing to make sure he's not released."

"I don't usually go to parole—" She stopped short, her eyes widening. "I can't believe I didn't think of this before. There was a perp I put away for viciously beating his girlfriend and her daughter." She dropped her gaze to the phone. "Gabe, check out Martino Hovel. See what he's been up to."

"Hold on." More clicking of the keyboard in the background. "Martino Hovel died in prison last year. Apparently, a blood vessel burst in his brain."

"That counts him out." She grimaced. "I guess we'll just work with the few names we have."

"Let me know if you need anything else," Gabe said. "Rhy told me I should help you when I can."

"We will," Jina assured him.

"Thanks again," Cole added, before reaching over to push the end button. "It's good that we have a place to start."

"Yes, I'm glad to have some names. But it doesn't seem logical that either Rinko or Navarro would come after me so many months after they got out. I mean, why would they bother now?"

"I don't know." He tapped the computer where he'd taken note of the names. "Let's focus on Terry Straub who is up for parole."

"Okay." She leaned forward, propping her elbows on the table. "We can do computer work on these guys for now, but we need to talk about how to draw this guy out."

And here it is, he thought with a sigh. "Draw him out?"

"Yes." Her blue eyes gleamed. "I think we should ask some of the members of my tactical team to stake out the strip mall. We'll head over there at dusk. You can stay in the car, while I get out and start looking around. When this guy tries to take another shot at me, we'll grab him."

"Have you lost your mind?" He didn't bother to hide his exasperation. "What if he hits and kills you before anyone sees him?"

She waved that off. "My teammates are great. I trust them with my life. They'll have the place staked out for at least an hour before we head out."

He didn't doubt the skills of her team, but the plan was reckless just the same. "Let's try to make some headway on these suspects, first. Maybe we can go after this guy rather than waiting for him to show up at the strip mall."

After a pause, she shrugged. "Okay, fine. But if we don't find anything in an hour, I'm going to make some calls. I'm sure I can get a handful of my teammates to head over."

"The Brookland PD will not be happy to find out we're setting up a sting operation on their turf," he warned.

"Maybe not, but Rhy lives in Brookland. I'm sure he'll help smooth things over." She flashed a grin. "I almost dropped his name today with Irving but figured I should wait until we really need the higher-level support."

He managed to smile back, despite his annoyance. "Good call."

They spent over an hour digging into Terrance Straub. The guy only had one brother who was also in jail. His parents were divorced and had moved to different cities. After an exhaustive search of tracking Straub's former friends on social media, they'd come up empty-handed. Based on the posts he'd seen, it didn't seem as if any of them cared if the guy was released from jail or not.

"One down and two more to go," she said, rubbing her eyes. "I'd rather stake out a crime scene than spend my days staring at a computer."

He could understand that Jina was a woman of action,

not one for sitting and painstakingly reviewing evidence. "It's not glamorous. Let's try Rinko first."

"Okay. But we might need food. I can't believe I'm saying this after Rosie's huge breakfast, but I'm hungry."

"I can throw in a pizza," he offered, surprised by the late afternoon hour. It hadn't seemed like they'd been working for so long, but they'd gotten a late start thanks to the fire followed by breakfast, then the gas station shooting. Especially the ridiculously long interview with the Brookland detectives. "Do you like your pizza loaded with the works?"

"Yes." She grabbed her phone from the charger. "I'm texting my teammates. I'm sure they'll be able to meet us at the strip mall later."

"I don't like that plan." He reached for the freezer, then stopped when he glanced through the small kitchen window in time to see a black vehicle driving past his house. "Jina? Is that the Honda?"

"Where?" She jumped from her seat to join him. "I can't tell if there's a license plate or not. Let's head outside, we'll know for sure it's the shooter if he drives past your house again."

"Okay." He prayed he was overreacting. He gestured to the back door. "We'll split up, taking each side of the house."

"I'll go right, you go left," she said with a nod.

He went out first, taking the left-hand side of his house, leaving her to go along the other side. His neighbors were relatively close, and he suspected Ida Potter would be watching out her window. The only good part about Ida's nosiness was that she wouldn't hesitate to call the police if things went sideways.

Once he was in a position where he could see the road, he hunkered down to wait. His patience was soon rewarded. The black Honda appeared from the same direction it had taken before, as if the driver had simply gone around the block.

"Stop! Police!" Hearing Jina's shout, he quickly ran out from his hiding spot. The driver of the SUV hit the gas, speeding away like the coward he was.

This time, he had noticed the driver was white and wore a black ball cap. But the worst part was that the shooter knew where he lived.

He needed to get Jina out of there ASAP.

CHAPTER SEVEN

Jina sprinted toward the disappearing car, despite knowing it was a useless endeavor. The black Honda careened around the corner at a dangerously fast rate of speed, and while she cut through lawns, it was no use.

The Honda disappeared from her line of sight.

Swallowing a curse—giving up swearing had never been so difficult—she bent at the waist to catch her breath. What was up with this guy? Why risk driving by Cole's house in broad daylight?

Then she straightened, realizing the shooter shouldn't have known where Cole lived in the first place. Not good. She turned to jog back as Cole headed toward her.

"Did you get a look at him?"

"No. Although Gabe was right about the ball cap." She hurried forward. "I'd like to know how he found your address."

"Me too." He scowled. "Let's go. We can't stay here."

She hated to admit he was right. Using Cole's home to set herself up as bait wouldn't work. Mr. Glen's duplex had already been damaged, she didn't want to add Cole's house to the mix. Especially since he had neighbors on each side.

Besides, the shooter should know they wouldn't stay now that they'd seen him.

"Fine, let me get my phone." She wasn't leaving it behind this time.

Cole disappeared into his bedroom, likely to pack a bag. She was glad she still had hers in his vehicle. Tucking the phone into her pocket, she watched the street out front to make sure the black Honda didn't double back.

This perp was not acting like the typical shooter. Not just because he'd set fire to Mr. Glen's duplex, but all this driving around, firing at them in the middle of the day? It was almost as if this guy had a sense of urgency driving him to violence.

Why, she couldn't imagine. Criminal profiling was not her strong suit. She preferred to aim and shoot.

She'd been tempted to fire at the SUV but had held back. Mostly because shooting a moving vehicle wasn't as easy as it looked on TV. And neither was shooting and hitting what you were aiming at while running.

The most important reason, though, was not having probable cause. The driver had only gone past the house twice. That wasn't a crime. She couldn't take out a perp's vehicle because he *might* commit a crime. No matter how much she wanted to.

Cole joined her in the kitchen. He grabbed the laptop from the table and stuck that into his duffel bag. "Ready?"

"Yes." She grimaced. "I hate to say it, but your vehicle has been compromised. We need a rental."

"I agree." He tossed his bag into the back seat beside hers. "I'd like to know how he found us here."

She shared his concern. "There's a car rental place in Brookland that Rhy has used on several occasions."

He shot her a curious look. "Why would a police captain need to rent cars?"

"Oh, for some reason our team seems to attract trouble, and our vehicles often sustain damage." She slid into the passenger seat. "It's almost funny if you think about it."

Cole shot her a look that clearly said he wasn't laughing. Understandable since she was the target of this mess. One he'd inadvertently gotten himself mixed up in.

"You know, you can drop me off at the car rental. No need for you to be involved moving forward." She should have cut him loose before now. "I'll get my teammates to help me out. You should return to your cold case investigation."

"No." His blunt response surprised her. "I've been fired upon too. He knows where I live. I'm part of this whether you like it or not."

"I'm sorry. I know this is my fault." She felt bad for dragging him into her—whatever this was. "All the more reason we need to set up a sting operation using me as bait to draw this guy out."

"Give it up, Jina." He sounded weary. "Let's focus on getting a rental. After that, we need to find a place to stay and get something to eat. Not necessarily in that order."

Her stomach was rumbling, so she wasn't going to argue about grabbing something for dinner. And she knew of a few places where they could stay.

"Can you call your fellow Peabody police officers to have them swing by to keep an eye on your place?"

He shrugged. "I could, but that's not a good use of resources. We don't know the shooter will return."

"I know, but I'll feel bad if he sets your house on fire."

"He won't." He shot her a quick glance. "The only reason he did that at the duplex was because he thought you were home."

That was probably true. Yet it didn't make her feel any better. "The longer you stick with me, the more likely you'll get hurt." Oddly, she didn't like the idea of Cole being in danger because of her. Normally, she considered cops as equals, perfectly capable of holding their own in tight spots and keeping themselves safe.

So why this strange desire to protect Cole? He didn't need her protection, and vice versa.

Too much togetherness. They'd spent most of the day together, and that was highly unusual for her. She gave herself a mental shake as he pulled into the parking lot of the car rental facility.

They were working a case, not dating.

Fifteen minutes later, they were in a black Ford Bronco. She'd been able to use Rhy's name to get a discount, but the fee was still staggering.

"There's a motel in Brookland called the American Lodge," she said as Cole pulled out of the parking lot. "Gary, the owner, is a former firefighter who gives discounts to police and firefighters. They don't have room service, though, so we'll need to stop to pick up a pizza on the way."

"Sounds good." He glanced at her, then said, "You've stayed at the American Lodge before?"

"Not me, but just about everyone else on the team has." That wasn't entirely true, but the place had seen more than its fair share of action from the group over the past year. "Gary put in security cameras a while back, so that gives us an added advantage. Not that we should need to watch for the Honda now that we have new wheels."

"One motel is as good as another," he said with a shrug.

"The American Lodge is nice." She gestured to the right. "Head that way."

He followed her instructions. "There's a pizza place along the way, if that works."

"Perfect." She thumbed through her contacts to find Gary Campbell's number. Thankfully, he answered right away. "Hi, Gary, it's Jina from Rhy's tactical team."

"Hey, Jina, what's up? You need a room?"

"Yes, connecting rooms if you have them." She felt Cole's curious gaze but ignored it. She wasn't afraid he'd try anything hinky, Cole had been nothing but professional and was likely still in love with his dead wife, but she valued her privacy.

"You're in luck, the first floor connecting rooms are available."

"Thanks, Gary. We'll be there soon." She ended the call. "We're set."

"Okay." He shook his head. "I don't think I've ever heard of a motel putting in security cameras."

"Yeah, well, they've come in handy." She only hoped they wouldn't need to use Gary's cameras this time.

The way the shooter found them at Cole's house in Peabody nagged at her. This puzzle had too many missing pieces.

Once they'd eaten dinner, she'd reach out to Zeke, Flynn, and Cassidy for ideas on how to approach the strip mall as a location to draw the perp out.

Waiting around for the shooter to find them yet again wasn't an option.

COLE PAID FOR THE PIZZAS, then carried them out to the rental. He thought it was odd that a police tactical unit used a local motel often enough to know the owner by name and get a discount, then realized he may have underestimated what her team did on a regular basis.

"That smells amazing," Jina said when they were back on the road. "Maybe we should have gotten two of them."

He chuckled. "I did. Figured we could always eat cold pizza for breakfast if necessary."

There was a brief pause, before she replied, "Works for me."

A few minutes later, they reached the American Lodge, a long white two-story building not far from a church. It looked nicer than he'd expected.

"I'll get our rooms." Without waiting for a reply, she jumped out of the passenger seat. Since she knew the guy, he followed more slowly, letting her take the lead.

"The last two rooms on the ground floor." Gary slid two keys across the desk, eyeing him curiously. "I'm Gary."

"Cole Roberts. It's nice to meet you." He'd noticed Jina had paid with cash, which was also unusual. "We appreciate you accommodating our last-minute request."

"Any time." Gary waved that off. "My business has been booming between the Callahans, the Finnegans, and the rest of the tactical team. The only downside is when you guys draw danger that results in my building being damaged."

"Thanks, Gary, we won't let that happen." Jina flashed the motel owner a warm smile. "You're the best."

The tips of Gary's ears turned bright red at the compliment. "I'll keep an eye on the security cameras for you."

"Sounds good." She turned away to look at Cole. "Ready?"

"Yep." He held the door for her. "I was thinking we should park behind the building."

"I was going to suggest that too." She glanced at him. "You didn't see the black Honda behind us, right?"

"Correct." In truth, there were plenty of black Honda SUVs on the road, but all the ones he'd noticed had license plates.

Hopefully, their perp hadn't stolen a set to use. There hadn't been a front or rear plate when he'd driven past his house less than an hour ago, but the way things were going, he wouldn't put anything past the guy.

Jina opened one room, then propped the door open to unlock the other since he was carrying the two pizzas. "Open the connecting door on your side, okay?"

"Sure." He set the pizzas down on the small table, then did as she'd asked. Her side opened a second later.

"Let's eat if you don't mind." She brushed past him and opened the top box. "I don't mind cold pizza for breakfast, but it tastes better hot."

"I'd like to say grace." He squeezed past her to sit at the table beside her. "We have a lot to be thankful for."

"Ah, okay." She flushed and bowed her head.

On impulse, he took her hand in his. "Dear Lord Jesus, we thank You for this food we are about to eat. We also thank You for keeping us safe in Your care. Amen."

"Amen." He was surprised she'd echoed the prayer. She sent him a wry glance, then gently tugged her hand from his to reach for the pizza. "As Roscoe would say, dig in."

He chuckled and helped himself to a slice of the pie loaded with the works. For long minutes, they ate in silence, enjoying the gooey cheese and zesty sauce.

All too soon, she ruined the companionable mood.

"Let's talk about the strip mall. I really think this perp will expect us to show up there tonight."

Which was a good reason to stay away, but he didn't voice his thought. "I don't see how we can safely set you up as bait in an area that's wide open."

"It can work if my teammates get out there first to get in position." She tapped on her phone screen while eating. "We'll talk to Zeke, see what he thinks."

He didn't doubt her teammates' skills as cops, but sacrificing Jina's safety was not happening. "Maybe you should ask Zeke and the others to check the place out first to see if it's a reasonable location. If not, there may be another angle to approach this."

She glanced at him, then nodded. "Okay, I can go along with that. But if they like the strip mall, no complaining."

"Fine." He didn't like it and silently prayed that these teammates of hers would agree with him that the strip mall wasn't a viable option.

Not that he could come up with a better one. And that was the crux of the matter. She was right in that they needed a place where this guy would try to come find them.

Preferably not a well-populated location like the neighborhood he lived in.

Her phone dinged. She smiled slightly as she texted back. "Zeke and Flynn will head over in about thirty minutes."

"Great." He would be happy to meet these guys in person. Hopefully, he could speak privately with one of them to voice his opinion that this was a lousy idea.

They polished off the first pizza by the time Jina's teammates arrived. The two guys eyed the second one with obvious longing, so he gestured to it. "Help yourselves."

"Hey, that was supposed to be our breakfast," Jina protested.

"Too bad," Zeke said, opening the box. "We haven't eaten all day thanks to a hostage situation that took hours to resolve."

"Yeah, thanks," Flynn added, his reddish hair a stark contrast to Zeke's black hair. "I wanted to stop on the way, but Zeke seemed to think you needed us right away."

"Fine." Jina threw up her hands. "Eat first, then we'll talk."

"Jesus, thank You for this food. Amen," Flynn said. It was the shortest prayer Cole had ever heard, and it made him smile at how the two men fell on the pizza like starving dogs.

"You might want to breathe," he said dryly. "Helps the digestion."

"Overrated," Zeke joked. Then he finished off the last slice and wiped his mouth with a napkin. "Okay, Jina, what's going on? Rhy said you've been targeted by gunfire and arson."

"Yep." She filled her teammates on the events of the past twenty-four hours. All hint of humor faded from their expressions as she described the recent danger. "We're not sure how they found us at Cole's place in Peabody. At first, we were thinking along the lines of perps I've put away who might be seeking revenge, but now I'm wondering if this guy has law enforcement background. He showed up at the gas station as if he'd suspected we would go there to view the video."

"If he's law enforcement, I'd think he'd be smart enough to avoid going to a place so close to the gym in the first place." Flynn looked at Cole. "Any chance you were followed from the gas station to your home?"

"I watched for a tail, but it's possible I missed one in the steady stream of traffic. And really, if this guy is a member of the gym, maybe he recognized me and figured out where I lived from some other source." Cole shrugged, then added, "Unfortunately, we have more suspects than not."

"The gym attack brings us to the strip mall," Jina said, picking up the thread. "That area behind the strip mall is where he tried to run me over."

"This guy is a menace," Zeke said with a dark frown.

"Tell me about it," Cole agreed. "But here's the part where Jina and I are not on the same page. She wants to head back to that strip mall later tonight to see if the shooter returns."

"I can see why," Flynn said.

That was not what Cole wanted to hear. "It's dangerous, not to mention there aren't that many places for those of you backing her up to hide. This guy might hit her this time."

"I have extra tactical gear in my trunk," Zeke offered. "It won't be specifically fitted for you, Jina, but it should work well enough."

What was wrong with these two? Did they really think having Jina expose herself to this nutcase was a good idea? He fought to keep his tone level. "I think you need to head out to look at this strip mall before you move forward with any sort of plan."

"We can do that," Flynn agreed. He stood and bent the empty pizza box in half. "Come on, Zeke. Let's check it out."

"I have a list of Mike's gym members that we need to look at," Cole said, mostly to prevent Jina from tagging along with the guys. "I'd like your opinion on them."

"Okay." She walked with Zeke and Flynn to the door.

"Let me know what you guys think after you scope the place out."

"Will do." Zeke headed outside with Flynn following behind him.

Over Jina's shoulder, he swept his gaze over the parking lot. Everything looked quiet and serene. For now.

"Let's check the list of names." Jina was all business after the guys left. "I'd like to get that finished before we head out to the strip mall."

He found himself grinding his molars together at her assumption. Without saying anything, he wiped the table with a napkin, then set up his laptop. She sat right next to him to see the screen.

Close enough to kiss, not that he'd be stupid enough to consider such a thing.

After bringing up his email program, he clicked on the attachment Mike sent. The list of names was shorter than he'd anticipated.

"Ten names, huh?" Jina mused, her eyes on the screen.

"Yeah." He turned the laptop so she could see it better. "Any of them look familiar?"

She took her time, then nodded. "Oliver Norman. He was one of the guys who hit on me. I only know his name because his buddy egged him on by saying, 'Yeah, Oliver, go for it.'" She turned to look at him. "I don't know his buddy's name, but both of them stayed far away from me after I put Oliver down."

"Looks like Oliver is a cop." Mike had helpfully added an occupation to each name as he knew it. "Any other names seem familiar? If not, we'll start with our good friend Ollie."

She chuckled at the nickname, then looked back at the screen. "No. Most of the guys I sparred with didn't tell me their names. It's probably best to start with Ollie and go from there."

The first thing he did was check Oliver Norman's criminal record. Finding nothing there, he switched gears. "Let's hope Oliver Norman has a social media presence."

"I don't get why he would," Jina murmured. "Not only is it a total waste of time, but why would you make it easier for people to find you?"

"I don't get it either." Renee had been on social media to keep in touch with her numerous cousins scattered across the country, but it had been a nightmare for him to get the account closed after her passing. "Huh. Here's an Oliver Norman who lives in Timberland Falls."

"He drives out of his way to go to Mike's," Jina said, leaning forward to see better. "Yep, that's him. Except he wasn't smiling like that when I saw him last."

"You enjoyed every minute of putting him down, didn't you?"

"I can't lie, it was satisfying." Her smile faded. "It's not that I wanted to be confrontational, but what is it about a woman working out alone at a gym that makes men think she's there to be picked up? I mean, seriously, I couldn't have looked any worse all hot, red-faced, and sweaty."

"You're beautiful no matter what. And men are simple creatures. I could tell those guys couldn't seem to resist trying to impress a pretty girl."

"Idiots," she muttered half under her breath. She gave him a sideways glance. "You never tried."

"Nope." He had to tear his gaze away from her mouth. Despite his attempt to remain professional, it seemed he was a simple creature too.

Pretty girl plus attraction equals kiss.

Yeah, he was an idiot all right. He needed to stay

focused on the task at hand. He scrolled through Oliver's social media page. "I don't see any postings related to Mike's gym."

"Why would he? He's too arrogant to put something like that out there into the world for all to see. Hold on, see that guy?" She tapped her index finger on the picture. "That's his buddy."

"Evan Wilde," he read out loud. He toggled back to the document Mike had sent. "Wilde is on here. He's a cop."

"Great, I guess that was my lucky day," she groused.

Evan Wilde also came up clean as far as a criminal record, and he lived in Timberland Falls too. That gave him another idea. "Let's see if either of these guys has a black Honda registered to their name."

Jina's phone pinged with an incoming text. As he accessed the DMV database, she read it out loud. "Strip mall is deserted. Not sure this will work. Be back soon."

He refrained from saying I told you so. He felt certain they were onto something with Oliver, but that thought was short-lived.

"Neither guy drives a black Honda SUV." He scowled, wondering if they'd borrowed or stolen the car. "We have their addresses. It might be worth it to head over in the morning to meet with them face-to-face."

"I still think we should try the strip mall." Her expression was stubborn. "It's not completely dark yet, so there's time for the guys to get in position before the main event." She waved at the screen. "I'm not sure either of these guys is the shooter. They are obviously friends who hang out together. If one was angry enough to fire a weapon at me, I feel the other would be right there with him, riding shotgun. They come across like pack animals where I see our shooter as a loner. We'll have better luck with the strip mall."

Their shooter being a loner was a valid point. But going to the strip mall was foolish. He strove to keep his tone even. "If Zeke and Flynn aren't sold on the location, it's a no-go."

"They didn't say no, they said they'd come back here to talk about it." She sat back in her seat, crossing her arms over her chest. "Come on, Cole. I'd think you'd want to get this over and done with so you can get back to your cold case."

As if on cue, his phone rang. Seeing the ME's name on the screen, he quickly answered. "This is Detective Roberts."

"Detective, you'll be glad to know I have verified the dental records on the skeletal remains of your victim," Dr. Swain said. "I'm glad you asked us to check the skull X-rays with the dental records of your missing person."

He straightened in his chair, unable to look at Jina. "They're a match?"

"Indeed, they are. We have positively identified the skeletal remains as Bradley Crow."

The news shouldn't have been a shock, but it was. He'd been so distracted by the current gunman attacking Jina that he'd pushed all thoughts of Crow to the back of his mind. "That's great work."

"Thanks, but that is my job," Dr. Swain said modestly. "And you pointed us in the right direction. That being said, I assume you'll be notifying Mr. Crow's parents?"

"Yes, I'll do the death notification." He glanced at his watch, realizing it wasn't too late to head out to do that now. It would be one way of getting around Jina's plan to head to the strip mall.

Yet he also knew she'd simply go without him.

"Let me know if you need anything else," Dr. Swain

was saying. "I highly doubt they'll want to view his remains."

"Probably not, but I'll let you know. Oh, one more thing," he said, before the ME could end the call. "Did you verify how long the bones had been buried?"

"Yes, I would estimate eleven to twelve years."

"Thank you, Doctor." He lowered his phone and looked at Jina. From the stricken expression on her face, he could tell she had overheard the news.

News that changed everything. Whether he liked it or not, Jina had to be considered a suspect in Bradley Crow's murder.

CHAPTER EIGHT

Her stalker was the dead man found buried on her parents' farmland. The flash of guilt in Cole's eyes convinced her that he was one step away from arresting her.

"I didn't kill him." She couldn't quite hide the hint of desperation in her tone. "And you have no proof that I did."

"There is plenty of circumstantial evidence pointing toward you," he said in a low voice. "And I want to believe you, but if you didn't bash his head in, who did?"

"Isn't it your job to figure that out?" The moment she said the words, she wanted to take them back. She tried again. "You mentioned doing the death notification to his parents. I assume you'll interview them at the same time. Crow must have had friends, someone who knew him on a personal level."

He watched her for a moment as if trying to decide how to respond. Hearing car doors slamming outside, she stepped toward the window to see that Zeke and Flynn had returned.

Crossing to the door, she let them in.

"I have a call out to Cassidy; she's on her way," Zeke

said upon entering the room. "Using the strip mall isn't a great place for a trap, we need at least four of us to cover each side to make it work."

When Cole didn't say anything, she assumed he was taking himself out of the mix, so she reached for her phone. "Okay, we have Cassidy, now let's try Steele, Brock, or Grayson. Roscoe is on his honeymoon, but I'm sure one of the others will join us."

"I need to head to Peabody for a death notification," Cole said with a frown. "If you wait for me to get back, I'm happy to be your fourth."

She sent him a sideways glance, trying to judge if he was serious. "Thanks, but we have this covered. You have a job to do and so do we."

His frown deepened into a scowl. "I'd rather you wait for me."

She would rather he go away and leave the matter of the shooter to the tactical team, but she managed to bite her tongue. Obviously, Cole wanted to stay close because he'd be taking her into custody at some point in the not-so-distant future.

Like first thing tomorrow morning.

Her stomach twisted painfully, but she refused to show any sign of weakness. She knew she hadn't bashed Bradley's head in. She had fired that shot, then followed his blood trail until it disappeared.

Yes, she should have notified the police.

But she hadn't. And that decision haunted her now.

"What's up?" Steele's voice echoed in her ear.

"Hey, Steele, I'm being targeted by a gunman. Zeke, Flynn, and Cassidy are heading here to the American Lodge. We need another cop to help with the stakeout. Are you interested?"

"Absolutely. I can be there in twenty."

Humbled by her team's willingness to jump in to assist, she smiled. "Great, thanks. There's a strip mall tucked behind the MMA gym. I'm hoping to goad the shooter into taking another try at me."

"Does Rhy know about this?" Steele asked.

"No." She found herself holding her breath, fearing Steele would back out.

"Okay. Be there soon."

When Steele ended the call, she turned to her colleagues. "He's on his way."

Zeke and Flynn exchanged a glance and nodded. "Sounds good," Zeke said.

"We're going to head back to the strip mall to settle in," Flynn added. "I'll text both Cassidy and Steele to meet us there."

"Good. I'll need to borrow one of your cars to head over. Mine was towed to a local garage, so I don't have my own ride." She managed a smile. "Hopefully, this guy will show. I'm anxious to take him down."

"And if he doesn't?" Cole asked.

She shrugged. "We can try again tomorrow. But I think he'll come tonight."

"Use my truck." Zeke tossed her the keys.

"We'll be in touch." Flynn gave her a nod, then he and Zeke went out to his car, leaving the pickup truck behind.

A long, heavy silence stretched between her and Cole once the guys were gone. He took a step toward the door, paused, then turned back to her. "I'd like your phone number so I can text you when I'm on my way back."

Her gut instinct was to refuse since it wasn't her job to make it easier for him to arrest her. A moot point, really, since he already knew where to find her. "Okay." She gave him the number, watching as he typed it into his phone.

"Thanks." He held her gaze for a long moment. Then he took a step toward her and reached for her hand. She was so surprised she didn't resist. "I don't think you killed Crow, but I'm going to need your help to prove that."

His statement caught her off guard. "You believe me?"

With a sigh, he nodded. "I do. But I doubt my lieutenant will share my viewpoint, so the sooner we figure out who did kill him and why, the better."

"We?" She regarded him thoughtfully. Trusting men wasn't easy for her, but for some odd reason, she believed him. "Okay. I can go along with that idea."

"Good." Still holding her hand, he stepped closer and brushed a kiss along her cheek. "Please stay safe until I can get back."

The sweet caress ridiculously made her heart race. "I'll be fine."

"I'm counting on that." Releasing her hand, he headed outside. Alone in the room, she felt a strange sense of loss. Having spent the better part of the past twenty hours with Cole Roberts, she was disconcerted to realize she missed him.

A man she barely knew. A detective who would more likely than not arrest her in the next day or so.

Why now? she thought wearily, dragging her hands through her hair. Why was she keenly aware of the one guy who was so wrong for her?

This wasn't the time to be distracted by a good-looking man. She was immune to that sort of thing or was until now.

Glancing at her phone, she realized the rest of her team wouldn't need her for at least another thirty minutes or so. Crossing to Cole's computer, she dropped into the chair to pick up where they'd left off digging into the guys on Mike's list.

It was either do something or go crazy. She preferred action, but a computer search would have to do.

Yet her mind wandered back in time to that fateful night when she'd heard the sound of her bedroom window opening. Replaying the sequence of events, she knew with absolute certainty she had only wounded the intruder's arm. Was that enough to have caused him to stumble and fall, hitting his head on a rock?

And if so, who had buried him?

It didn't make sense, but stranger things had happened.

Squashing the temptation to call Shelly, she forced herself to search social media. They'd found Oliver and Evan, but she didn't think either of them was the shooter/arsonist.

With painstaking slowness, she moved on to the next name. She was only halfway through when her phone buzzed with an incoming text from Zeke.

We're ready.

About time! She jumped out of the chair and dug in her pocket for Zeke's truck keys. Darkness had fallen, but there was a light outside each of the motel rooms. She crossed the parking lot, unlocking Zeke's truck with the key fob. She took a moment to pull the spare vest from Zeke's back seat. Covering her torso would have to be good enough. Head shots were extremely difficult to make, and cops were taught to aim for center mass.

If this guy was a cop, that's what he should do. Although he hadn't come very close that first night outside the gym.

The truck key fob slipped from her hand, and as she bent to pick it up, a gunshot rang out.

What in the world? Dropping to her knees, she reached for her weapon and scanned her surroundings. How had the shooter found her there?

The lights along the front of the motel made it difficult to see. She avoided them, searching for the assailant. Another gunshot ripped through the air, pinging off Zeke's truck.

He must be somewhere near the trees.

"Who's sorry now?" The male voice was low and full of spite. It was the first time the perp had said anything, and she wasn't sure if that was a good thing. Edging along the side of the vehicle, she tried to pinpoint his location. Then she had to duck back behind the truck when another gunshot rang out.

It was almost as if this guy knew she was alone! How long had he been out there watching the motel? Long enough to see Zeke, Flynn, and Cole all leave?

There was nothing worse than being on the defensive. She made herself small, hoping Gary had heard the gunfire and was calling it in.

Her plan to draw the shooter had worked, but not in the way she'd intended.

She only hoped she could hold him off long enough for her backup to arrive.

COLE SAT in the living room of Mr. and Mrs. Crow. To his critical eye, they didn't look shocked or horrified upon learning of their son's death.

"He's been gone a long time," Erma Crow said in a low voice. "We figured something bad had happened to him."

"Where did you find him?" Henry Crow asked.

Cole chose his words carefully. "His body was uncovered by construction workers here in Peabody. Do you know of anyone who would do something like this? Did your son have enemies?"

"None that I know of," Erma said, without looking at her husband. "He was a nice boy. Didn't like school much, but he worked hard at the bar."

When Henry didn't expound on that, Cole asked, "Where did you think he'd gone twelve years ago? Had he mentioned wanting to travel?"

This time, they exchanged a quick look as if gauging how much to say.

"Look, I can't find out what happened to your son if you don't tell me what you know." Cole added a note of steel to his tone. "I need your cooperation. At the time you reported him missing, three months after you last saw him, you told the detective on the case that you thought your son went to Madison to find a new job." He'd stopped in at the precinct on his way here to get the former detective's file on the missing person case.

"I, uh, yes." Erma shot a guilty look at Howard. "We had a disagreement with Brad over his taking over as bar manager. We didn't think he was ready for that level of responsibility."

A wave of relief hit hard. An argument between Brad Crow and his parents opened them up as possible suspects too. "How long after your disagreement did you notice your son was missing?"

Erma chewed her lower lip. "We, uh, thought Brad was staying with a friend."

"Which friend?" That detail had not been in the initial report, making him think they were making it up. "I'd like to chat with him or her."

"Wade Adams," Erma said. "We called Wade before notifying the police to report him missing, but Wade hadn't seen him. Wade lived here in Peabody at the time."

He jotted the name down, secretly thrilled to have another potential suspect in Brad's murder. "Anyone else? Did your son have a girlfriend?"

"Not that I know of," Erma replied. "He dated a few different girls, but none were serious."

"Do you have their names?" he pressed.

"Oh, that was such a long time ago." Erma's hands twisted in her lap. "I don't recall their names."

"What about you, Mr. Crow?" He looked directly at Henry. "Do you know of any girlfriends or other friends that I can get in touch with?"

"I worked long hours at the bar," the older man said bluntly. "I didn't pay any attention to Brad's friends, female or otherwise."

"Why did you wait three months to notify the police?"

"You have to understand, Brad was an adult." Erma's expression was pained. "He could do what he wanted. We assumed he'd moved in with Wade and had gotten a different job. Then we thought he must have moved to a new city."

He wasn't sure he bought their story. Most parents would still maintain contact even after a fight, wouldn't they? "Do you still own the bar?" He asked the question, despite already knowing the answer.

"No, we sold it early last year," Henry said. "We barely scraped by during the pandemic, and to be honest, I was tired of working so many hours. I drive a school bus now, and Erma cleans houses. We make ends meet."

Staring at his notebook, trying to come up with additional questions, a strange wave of apprehension washed over him. Instantly, he thought of Jina and her decision to head out to the strip mall. It was tempting to rush through this to join her, but he forced himself to make sure he'd covered all the bases.

"Why did you assume Brad had headed to Madison?" he asked. "Did he know someone there? Maybe a former classmate?"

"Oh, uh," Erma faltered, glancing at Howard. "I don't remember if Brad specifically mentioned Madison or if that's just where we assumed he'd go. It's a much bigger city than Peabody."

So was Milwaukee, which was closer. Brad's parents weren't being nearly as helpful as he'd anticipated. He watched Erma closely, wondering if she'd known or suspected her son had been stalking Jina and possibly other young women too. If he could prove that the guy had been a stalker, his suspect pool would widen exponentially.

"Do you have any of Brad's personal things here? I'd like to go through them."

"We got rid of Brad's things a long time ago," Henry said bluntly. "He didn't have much, and there was no reason to keep them."

Again, he found that odd. He hadn't gotten rid of Renee's clothing for a solid year after her death, and he'd known she wasn't coming back. Would a parent really toss the only items their missing son had left behind? Especially when they didn't know whether he was alive or dead?

"I really need you both to think back to those days before Brad disappeared. Even a small detail may help me figure out what happened to him."

"How did he die?" Erma asked. He was a little surprised it had taken her so long to ask. "Was it some sort of accident?"

"I'm sorry, but I can't say for sure what happened to your son. It could have been an accident, or someone may have hurt him on purpose." He watched Erma's expression closely. "That's why I need to know the names of his friends and enemies."

There was another long pause as they mulled this over. Finally, Erma spoke up. "Our bar manager at the time was Ian Muller. I don't think he and Brad were enemies exactly, but I know Ian wasn't happy when he heard Brad wanted his job."

"Ian wouldn't hurt Brad," Henry protested. "He knew his job was secure."

"Where is Ian Muller now?" he asked, jotting the name in his notebook. "Does he still work the bar?"

"Yes, of course." Erma seemed surprised by this question. "Ian and his wife, Amy, bought the bar from us."

"Okay, thank you." He tucked his notebook away and drew out a business card. "Please call me if you think of anything else. I really need to find out who did this to your son."

Erma took the card. "Thank you, Detective."

The older couple followed him outside. Sliding in behind the wheel, he considered heading out to the bar to talk to Ian Muller. At this time of the night, the place would still be open. Yet concern for Jina overruled his common sense.

He headed back toward Brookland, using the hands-free function in the rental SUV to send a text.

R U at strip mall?

There was no response for several long minutes, making him believe she was indeed at the strip mall doing her best to draw the shooter out. But then a response came through.

Perp at AL.

What? The shooter was at the American Lodge? How in the world had that happened? He hit the gas, sending the SUV surging forward. She couldn't be hurt too badly if she'd texted him back, but just thinking of that, a flash of apprehension had him desperate to see her.

To hug her.

Mentally kicking himself for leaving her in the first place, he took advantage of the light traffic on the interstate to zip down the left lane, easily topping fifteen miles over the posted speed limit to reach the American Lodge.

His heart just about thumped out of his chest when he saw not one but three sets of red and blue lights flashing in the darkness.

Braking to an abrupt halt, he shot out of the car and waded into the sea of police officers milling about. Spotting Jina, he hurried to her side. "Are you okay?"

"Fine." She scowled. "Zeke's truck took several slugs, though."

"Zeke was here?" He noticed Zeke and Flynn were standing beside a tall man with dark hair, whom he assumed was Steele and a pretty redhead who must be Cassidy.

"No, all four of my teammates were at the strip mall." Her voice was laced with disgust. "I was here alone. I came out to Zeke's truck to head over when I accidentally dropped his keys. That's when the first shot rang out."

He should have been there. Swallowing hard, he tried to sound calm. "I'm so glad you're not hurt. I know God was watching over you."

She shrugged. "Maybe."

The wave of apprehension could have been when the first shot had been fired. Although why he would feel something was off so far away from Jina was strange. He believed in God and that Jesus had died to save them, but he wasn't one to buy into the woo-woo stuff. Maybe the apprehension had been his imagination. As much as he'd tried to focus on the case of Brad Crow, he'd been worried about Jina.

Which brought him back to the immediate threat. "Did you get a good look at him?"

"No, it was too dark, and he was in the trees." She glowered at the trees in question. "But I have Gary going through his security cameras to see if any of them picked him up."

"Good idea." It irked him to know that Gary's security cameras hadn't prevented the attack on Jina, but a picture of this perp would help.

"He said something this time," Jina continued. "He asked, 'Who's sorry now?'"

Who's sorry now? "Does that phrase ring a bell?"

"Not really." Her gaze looked thoughtful.

"Jina?" A tall man with short blond hair strode into the parking lot with an air of authority. "Fill me in."

"Captain." Jina straightened her spine as she turned to face her boss. He'd heard about Rhy Finnegan but had never met him. "I was heading out to meet with Zeke, Flynn, Steele, and Cassidy when I was targeted by gunfire here at the American Lodge. The perp fired three shots in total, hitting Zeke's truck twice from what I can see. I didn't see him clearly but have requested Gary to review his security video."

"And why exactly were you meeting with Zeke, Flynn, Steele, and Cassidy?" Rhy asked.

Before Jina could answer, Zeke spoke up. "We were checking the strip mall for signs of the perp. Something the locals may have missed."

Rhy looked from Zeke back to Jina as if waiting for her response.

"That's only part of the story," Jina admitted. "It was my idea to surround the strip mall with officers to see if the perp might return. I thought if I presented myself at the location of a prior incident, the shooter would try again. Hence the vest." She tapped the body armor covering her chest. "Instead, he showed up here. I take full responsibility for my actions."

Her bold honesty was refreshing. Cole had the sense that if she'd claimed that all they were going to do was look for evidence, the rest of the team would have backed her up. Instead, she took accountability so that they wouldn't suffer because of her. The interaction reinforced to him that Jina had been telling the truth when she claimed she hadn't bashed Brad Crow over the head with a blunt object.

Yet believing her and proving her innocence were two completely different things.

"Thank you for telling me." Rhy nodded, then scanned the faces of the team members. "Next time, you'll want to keep me or Joe in the loop."

"Yes, sir!" all five tactical officers responded in unison.

Before Rhy could leave, Gary came outside, a resigned look on his face. "I have some video, but it's not helpful. I think this guy painted black stuff on his face because I don't have a single camera angle with a good image of his facial features."

"Figures," Flynn muttered.

"You'd think some guy walking around with black on his face would raise someone's suspicions," Cassidy said with a frown.

"You can take a look for yourself," Gary offered.

"Let's do it." Jina led the way inside the lobby.

Setting his laptop computer on the counter so they could all see, Gary showed them the various frames in which the shooter's image was captured. His face was covered with black, and the ball cap was pulled low on his forehead.

Not one offered anything remotely useful.

"I guess we're back at square one." Jina sounded defeated.

"Hey, don't give up," Zeke said. "We may get a match on the slugs pulled out of my truck. Maybe his weapon has been used in other crimes."

"I'm sorry about your truck, Zeke," Jina murmured.

"Don't sweat it." Zeke awkwardly patted her shoulder. "It's not the first time it's been shot up by a perp."

"It's not?" Cole stared at him. "Seriously?"

Zeke shrugged. "What can I say? Our team tends to be a magnet for trouble."

"No lie," Cassidy said with a grimace. "It's as if there's a black cloud hanging over us."

After a few more minutes, Rhy broke the silence. "Time to hit the road. There's nothing more we can do about this tonight. We'll regroup tomorrow."

It was an order, not a suggestion. On cue, the team dispersed. Jina glanced at Cole. "I guess we need to get out of here."

He was glad she was being reasonable about this. "Yes. We can find another place to stay for what's left of the night."

Outside, the officers were still inspecting the scene, which was centered around Zeke's truck. Imagining Jina huddled there as bullets whizzed by made his blood run cold. Using his key card, he accessed his room, with Jina following close behind.

"Did you get anything interesting from Bradley Crow's parents?" she asked as he packed up the laptop.

He was shocked by how badly he wanted to share the details of the interview with her. But that wasn't an option since she was a suspect too. "I did."

When he didn't elaborate, she sighed. "You won't tell me because I'm involved."

He straightened from the table, then took a step toward her. "I've already compromised this case by spending so much time with you."

She looked chagrined. "I know. I'm sorry."

"Don't apologize." He was the one who should have insisted she find a teammate to stay with rather than nominating himself for the job. "I'm so glad you weren't hurt. If anything had happened to you . . ." He didn't finish.

"I knew you'd blame yourself. But it was my idea. And I admit, he caught me off guard." Her gaze clung to his for a long moment. "There was one regret that nagged at me while I was waiting for my backup to arrive."

"Oh yeah? What's that?"

"This." She reached up to draw his head down and kissed him.

CHAPTER NINE

Jina wasn't sure why she'd thrown caution to the wind to impulsively kiss Cole. Yet the moment their mouths fused, all logical thought fled from her brain. Losing herself in Cole's embrace wasn't smart. But as the bullets were pinging off Zeke's truck, she'd told herself if she survived, she would kiss Cole.

And what a kiss it was. The impact sent her pulse into triple digits.

"Jina." His voice was low and husky as he broke off their kiss. "I—we can't."

For a moment, she'd forgotten she was still a suspect in Bradley Crow's murder. The realization popped the tiny balloon of hope in her heart. "Yeah, sorry. I—uh—"

A knock at the door interrupted them, which was probably a good thing. Drawing a deep breath to steady nerves that had gone haywire, she turned to open the door. Seeing Gary, she managed a smile.

"There hasn't been any damage to the rooms," she said quickly.

"That's good, but I'm just glad you're not hurt." Gary

glanced between her and Cole. "Did you want a copy of the video too? I sent one to Rhy, but I thought maybe you'd want one for yourself."

"Yes, please," Cole said. "I know there isn't much to see, but maybe the tech gurus can do something with the image."

"I agree. I'm sure Rhy send it to Gabe." She smiled at Gary. "Thanks for thinking of that. And don't worry, we're hitting the road soon."

"Okay." Gary looked relieved. "I'm sorry we didn't catch the shooter on the image before he fired at you."

"Not your fault," she quickly assured him. "I think he was hiding in the trees, biding his time before making a move."

"I'd like to know how he found you here," Cole said with a frown.

"I'm not sure, but we need to leave." She crossed to the table to grab Cole's laptop. He took it from her as she went into the connecting room to grab her bag.

Being on the run wasn't fun, and it gave her a new appreciation for what some of her teammates had been through over the past few months.

And how horrible it was to know someone you cared about was in the line of fire. Thankfully, Cole hadn't been there tonight, but if he had been? She hated to think about what might have happened.

Five minutes later, they were on the road. Cole glanced at her curiously. "Did that guy's voice sound familiar to you?"

She'd almost forgotten the guttural words the perp had uttered. "No, it didn't. And it's been bothering me that he asked, 'Who's sorry now?' Makes me think I must have apologized at some point. But when? And for what?" She shook her head. "I have no idea."

"I don't remember you apologizing for putting the guys at the gym down on the mat," he said.

"I may have, but if I did say sorry, I meant it as sarcasm. Not a real apology." She tried to think back. She didn't remember apologizing.

There was a moment of silence, before Cole asked, "Any ideas where to go next?"

"Oh, yeah. There's a motel that Roscoe used last month called the Wildflower Motel. It's nothing fancy, but it should do." She pulled her phone from her pocket, then powered it down.

"What's up with your phone?"

"Remember how you mentioned the perp must have assumed I was home when he started the fire at Mr. Glen's?" When Cole nodded, she continued. "I think you were right on the money. My phone was there, so he assumed I was too. I didn't have it at the gas station," she added. "But other than that, I've had the phone for all the other attempts he made against me."

"I see the logic, but I'm not sure how this guy can track your phone," Cole said.

"Who knows? Either way, I'm keeping it off until we can set up another sting operation."

"Wait a minute, what sting operation?" He sounded annoyed. "The last attempt blew up in your face."

"True, but that was before I thought of the possibility this guy can find my phone." Now that the idea had taken root in her mind, it blossomed. "Don't you see? This will work even better. I can station myself in a semi-secure location with my phone on, while the rest of you surround the property. You'll be ready when he makes his move, and we'll grab him. I am sure this will work."

"Famous last words," he said with a scowl.

She ignored that. "The key will be to find a place that's relatively isolated, so we don't put innocent lives at risk." Not a motel where there could be other customers in nearby rooms. Or a neighborhood. Something rural but not too far, or the perp might consider it a trap.

"And when exactly do you intend to do this?"

Glancing at her watch, she sighed. "It's too late to do that tonight, but we can work on it first thing tomorrow."

Cole didn't say anything for a long moment. He'd keyed in the Wildflower Motel and was heading west on the interstate per her suggestion. Then he finally asked, "You're going to talk to Rhy Finnegan about the plan first, right?"

"I guess I'll have to." She wasn't thrilled with the directive, but she wasn't going to risk her job either. "But not until we have a solid plan."

He sighed. "Fine. I'll help you with this if you do me a favor."

She tensed. "Like what?"

"I still need your help to find out who killed Bradley Crow."

She turned to look at him. "I thought you couldn't tell me about your interview with his parents."

He grimaced and nodded. "That's true. Doesn't mean I can't ask you a couple of questions, though."

"I'll do my best to answer them." She had hoped the interview with Brad's parents would somehow clear her, but obviously, it hadn't.

"I know." He eyed the rearview mirror frequently, clearly looking for a tail. "Do you recognize the names Wade Adams or Ian Muller?"

She rolled the names around in her mind. "I think Wade Adams was a few years ahead of me in high school. But the name Ian Muller doesn't sound at all familiar."

"Why do you remember Wade Adams and not Bradley Crow?" There was a hint of suspicion in his tone.

"Wade got into a fight one Friday night at a football game. The other guy, Tom Lightfoot, actually started it, thought Wade was ogling his girlfriend or something. A couple of the parents broke it up, but the police came and took them both away."

He nodded thoughtfully. "I'll double-check his arrest record, see if he's been involved with anything else, like drugs or burglary."

"You think Brad Crow knew Wade Adams?" She wondered if Brad Crow was also at that Friday night football game. If so, she hadn't noticed him. "That's interesting, but I'm not sure how it helps."

"Adams is someone to talk to, that's all," Cole said. Then he abruptly switched lanes and got off the interstate. The move was so fast she glanced over her shoulder, expecting to see the black Honda back there.

"We picked up a tail?"

"What? Oh, no." He flushed, then added, "I just remembered I needed to make a stop."

"A stop in Peabody?" She frowned. "We're heading back to your place?"

"No, a restaurant/bar." He hesitated for a long moment. "I shouldn't bring you with me, but I need to talk to Ian Muller, and he owns Peabody's Pub."

She had heard of the place but had never been there. Her parents only went out for special occasions, like their wedding anniversary, which was why they weren't home the night her stalker had sneaked into her room. "I heard they do a great fish fry."

"Too bad it's not Friday." He smiled. "This shouldn't take long."

"Fine with me." She was secretly glad to tag along for this interview. There had to be a way to prove she hadn't killed Crow. Shot at him, yes. Murdered him, no. "Did Ian Muller know Brad Crow?"

"Yes."

"And that makes him a suspect?" She wasn't sure why she was pushing for more information other than Cole had already crossed the line by spending time with her. Sure, he could argue that she was in danger, but she had her team-mates to use as backup, so his presence really wasn't needed.

Yet she was glad he intended to stay close. Not just because she appreciated his support, but more so because the zing of their kiss was still too fresh in her mind.

"That makes him a person of interest," Cole said. When he glanced at her, she understood.

Ian Muller was a person of interest exactly the way she was. Guilty until proven innocent.

COLE WAS BREAKING MORE rules than he could count. But that didn't change his determination not to let Jina go off on her own without him. Look at what happened at the American Lodge? Still, he understood her tagging along could jeopardize his case.

If he managed to find Crow's killer.

Jina wasn't a detective, but having her input as a fellow officer was valuable. At least, that was what he told himself.

Regardless, it was too late to turn the clock back now. He'd interviewed her because she'd lived on the farm where the body was found. Now he had little choice but to move forward with the investigation, praying he wasn't wrong about Jina.

And if he lost his job over this? Hiding a wince, he tried not to think about that.

After pulling into the parking lot of Peabody's Pub, he threw the gearshift into park and killed the engine. "Ready?"

"Yep." She pushed open her door. "Doesn't look too busy."

"Weeknight after the dinner rush." He shrugged. "That's the reason I decided to come now rather than wait until tomorrow."

"Smart move as we're going to be busy tomorrow setting up the new sting operation."

He reached the door first, holding it open for her. Stepping inside, he found the interior to be that of a typical pub. The bartender looked up with a smile as they approached. He quickly placed two drink napkins on the bar. "Welcome to Peabody's Pub. What can I get you?"

"Just ginger ale for me," Jina said. "Although I wouldn't mind some of your deep-fried cheese nuggets."

The bartender nodded. "And for you?"

"Same, we'll share the cheese nuggets." He took a seat, trying to ascertain if the bartender was Ian Muller. He didn't wear a name tag, but the guy's age of early to midforties was about right. He waited until the bartender had poured their soft drinks and placed their order for cheese curds, before asking, "Are you Ian Muller?"

The bartender looked at him in surprise. "Yes. I'm sorry, but I don't remember you."

"No, you wouldn't as we never met. My name is Cole Roberts, and this is Jina Wheeler. How long have you owned the place?"

"About eighteen months or so." Ian braced his arms on the bar, regarding them thoughtfully. "Why the question? Were you interested in buying it too?"

"No, nothing like that." Cole put some cash on the bar to cover their soft drinks and the appetizer in the event the conversation didn't go well. "I'd like to know when you last saw Bradley Crow."

Ian's spine straightened, and his gaze narrowed. "I had nothing to do with his disappearance."

"I didn't say you did." Cole kept his tone even. "But when did you see him last?"

"I have no clue, that was a long time ago." Ian frowned. "Who are you again?"

Cole pulled out his badge. "Peabody Detective Cole Roberts. I spoke earlier with Brad's parents. They mentioned their son wanted your job as the manager."

"Yeah, he did." Ian glanced down the bar at the other two patrons sitting there. Neither of them needed anything, so he turned back to Cole. "The kid was barely twenty and seemed to think he knew everything about running a pub. Which was funny since he was late for his shifts more often than not."

"Not a hard worker then," Jina murmured.

"Not even close," Ian said firmly. "Brad felt like he could get away with stuff because his parents owned the place. In a way, he did, but not when it came to moving up to the manager role."

"Do you know if Brad was friendly with anyone?" Cole asked. "Did he have a girlfriend?"

"Girlfriend?" Ian shook his head. "Not even in his

dreams. He was an odd duck, if you ask me. Awkward around people and not very friendly."

"And those traits would not be helpful in a manager role," Jina said, sipping her ginger ale.

"Exactly." Ian seemed to sense Jina was on his side. "I didn't have any respect for the kid, but that didn't mean I wanted him to take off like that, without warning. He never even said anything to his parents about leaving town."

"So they were surprised too?" he asked.

"Yes. When I mentioned his comment to me about taking over my job, his dad came right out and told me my position here was secure." Ian glanced down the bar again to make sure he wasn't needed. "Henry knew Brad wasn't manager material."

"I appreciate that insight," Cole said. "And you should know Mr. Crow told me the same thing."

"Good." Ian looked relieved.

A kid from the back came out with their deep-fried cheese nuggets. After setting them on the bar in front of them, he scurried back to the kitchen.

Jina helped herself. "Mmm. These are great."

"Thanks," Ian said with a smile. "That's a hot appetizer here. Sometimes we run out on busy nights."

"I can see why." She popped another nugget-sized deep-friend cheese ball into her mouth. "Did you ever notice Brad looking at the female patrons here?"

"Yeah, he looked," Ian admitted. "But so do a lot of guys, right?" He smiled at her. "Pretty women like you get lots of attention."

Jina narrowed her gaze, clearly warning him to back off. "I'm not looking for attention or compliments. I'm asking if Brad watched women in a lecherous way. As if he wanted something he knew he couldn't have. Or maybe in a way that made any of them feel uncomfortable. If he had, I'd think the woman in question would have complained."

Ian looked thoughtful for a minute. "Yes. There was one time a pretty girl came in with her parents. Brad must have been watching her much the way you described because her father went over to tell him to back off. At the time, Brad just shrugged and slinked back to the kitchen. But now that you mention it, he'd been intense."

Cole had to give Jina credit for coming up with this line of questioning. "That's good to know. Did he bother anyone else that you noticed? Female employees maybe?" He found himself hoping there were more suspects he could talk to.

"Nah. But I didn't pay that much attention. One of us had to work," Ian added. "And it wasn't going to be him."

"Did Brad give you any indication he was about to leave town?" Cole asked.

"No, the cops asked me that years ago. I honestly didn't think much of it when he didn't show up for work. As I said, he was always late. It wasn't until he'd missed the entire shift that me and his dad noticed he was gone."

Cole found that interesting too. Henry Crow wasn't coming across as being a concerned father. More like he was annoyed by his son and maybe glad that he'd taken off. "Anything else stick in your mind about the guy? Anything that could help us find him?"

"Not offhand. I'm surprised you're still looking for him after all this time." Someone waved, and Ian nodded to indicate he'd be right there. "Excuse me."

"I wonder if we could find that dad and his daughter," Jina murmured once Ian had moved down to refill drink orders. "Maybe Brad tried something there after they left the bar, and the dad reacted in kind."

"We can try, but if Ian doesn't remember their names,

I'm not sure how we'd track them down all these years later." He hated to admit the trip to Peabody's Pub hadn't been very helpful. Other than to convince him that Ian Muller probably hadn't killed the guy. Mostly because there was no motive. As Henry had mentioned, Ian wouldn't be threatened by Brad's desire to take over his job. Not when it was clear there was no chance of that happening.

He sampled the cheese nuggets and had to agree they were delicious. They were like mini mozzarella sticks. When Ian finished with the other patrons, he returned to check on them. "Another ginger ale?"

"No thanks. Do you remember the name of the father who told Brad off?"

Ian frowned. "No. I don't think they were locals. I don't recall seeing them after that." The pub owner shrugged. "Could be he came back at some point without the family, but if so, I don't remember."

"Okay, thanks." He tried to think of another question but was coming up blank. Lack of sleep and seemingly nonstop adrenaline had fried his brain.

Or maybe it was Jina's kiss that had done that. His heart rate still hadn't quite returned to normal after their brief and electric embrace. One that shouldn't have happened, despite how much he'd wanted it.

Either way, he decided it was time to end the interview. He pulled out a business card and slid it across the table. "I'd appreciate it if you'd call me if you remember anything else."

"Yeah, sure." Ian Muller took the card. "I hope you find him."

He hesitated, then decided the news would get out sooner or later. After all, Brad's parents knew the truth.

"We found his dead body. That's why I'm here asking questions."

Ian didn't look surprised by the news. "I always figured he'd gotten into trouble and had either been arrested or killed." He shook his head somberly. "I'm sorry for his parents. They're decent people."

That sparked another thought. "Did you ever see Henry fight with his son? Arguments that got loud or physical?"

"They argued, but it was never physical." Ian shrugged. "And most of the fights were about Brad not working hard, being late, or not working at all."

"Do you think it's possible Henry lost his temper and hit Brad?"

Ian grimaced. "I've never seen Henry lose his temper like that, but if you ask me, he didn't hold his son in high regard. Could he have lost it at home and slugged him? Yeah, sure. I'm just saying I've never seen it."

"Okay, that's helpful. Thanks." He added another ten-dollar bill to the cash on the table. "Again, if you think of anything else, please let me know."

Ian pocketed the cash, then made his way down the bar to interact with the other patrons.

He took another cheese nugget, smiling when he noticed Jina had eaten more than half of them.

When he glanced at her, she grinned. "Snooze, you lose. What can I say? I like them."

"Finish them up." He pushed the basket toward her. "We need to get back on the road."

Unrepentant, she popped the last nugget into her mouth. "What did you think of Ian?"

"He seems like a decent guy." He turned to face her. "What about you? I thought you might slap him when he called you pretty."

She wrinkled her nose. "He wears a wedding ring and shouldn't be flirting with me or anyone else. But aside from that, I agree with you. Difficult to imagine he'd have a reason to bash Brad's skull in." She drained her ginger ale, then waved her hand at the bar. "He has a good thing going here, and you can tell he is attentive to his customers. It's a nice place, maybe not super busy, but I'll bet that changes on weekends."

"Yeah. I don't think he's good for it either." Which left him with just Brad's parents and Jina as likely suspects. Maybe Wade Adams, too, depending on what the guy had to say once he found and interviewed him.

Something he needed to do sooner rather than later.

Tonight? Something to think about. He knew they'd be working most of the day tomorrow trying to set up Jina's sting operation.

After getting settled behind the wheel, he used his phone to do a quick search on Wade Adams. Disappointed, he quickly noted there were too many to know which Wade Adams was the guy he needed to talk to. It would take time to go through social media and other sites to find the Wade Adams that was the right age and had gone to Peabody High School. Oh, and who'd been arrested for disorderly conduct, which was the most likely charge that had been filed against him after the fight.

Then he brightened. The quickest way to get an image of the guy would be to check online for the Peabody High School yearbook. From there, he might be able to find a guy who looked a little similar on social media.

"Did you change your mind about heading to the Wild-flower Motel?" Jina asked.

"No. I was trying to find Wade Adams." He slid his phone into his pocket and started the rental. He backed out of the parking space, then headed back toward the interstate. "I thought his name was unique enough, but apparently not. I'll have to find his old yearbook photo first."

"I can help—" Her voice broke off as a crack of gunfire rang out, shattering his rear window.

"Down!" He wrenched the wheel into a tight right-hand turn to get out of the shooter's line of fire.

"No. Keep driving." To his shock and horror, Jina unbuckled her seatbelt and began to crawl into the back seat.

"Don't!" He didn't want her anywhere near the line of fire. "Keep your head down, Jina. He might shoot again!"

"That's fine. I need you to slow down, so we can draw him closer." Her voice was incredibly calm and infuriating. He understood what she was trying to do, but the risk was too great.

Then he was forced to take his foot off the gas pedal because of a parked car up ahead. Somehow, he managed to go around it without sideswiping it.

"Slower," Jina urged. A quick glance in the rearview showed Jina kneeling on the rear seat, holding her weapon in two hands. The only good thing about the missing window was that it offered her a clear view of the area behind them.

Swallowing hard, he did as she asked. But almost immediately the headlights of the vehicle behind him blinked off.

Then the vehicle disappeared altogether.

CHAPTER TEN

"Turn around! Don't let him get away! We need to find him!" Jina did not want to lose this shooter. "Hurry!"

"I don't think that's a good idea," Cole said tersely. "We need to get out of here."

"No! There are two of us and only one of him!" She would have grabbed his shoulders to shake him if she wasn't preoccupied with watching out the rear window. Or what used to be a window but was now open space. "We have the advantage!"

Cole turned the vehicle around. Yet he was moving too slowly for her peace of mind.

"I think he headed east." She had only gotten a glimpse of the vehicle as it turned away. No doubt the driver had understood that she would have taken him out and had decided to bail. "Take a right up at the next block."

Thankfully, Cole did as she requested. The street was empty. It was too late. This guy could be hiding anywhere.

She dropped her chin to her chest with despair. She hated being forced to play defense with this perp. Taking a deep breath, she turned and slid into a sitting position. "Never mind. He's gone."

"We need a replacement vehicle," Cole said, his gaze meeting hers in the rearview mirror. "And I'd really like to know how he found us here at the pub."

"I can't answer that." The way the perp had shown up was cause for concern. Then a thought occurred to her. "Pull over. Maybe he put a GPS tracker on the car."

"And when would he have done that?" Cole asked, as he pulled into the parking lot of a local business. "He found you at the American Lodge without the rental being there."

"It was there earlier, though." She jumped out of the back seat, then leaned in to ask, "Do you have a flashlight?"

"Only my phone." He turned the flashlight app on, then handed it to her. "Do you know what you're looking for?"

"I hope I'll know it when I see it." GPS trackers came in all shapes and sizes. Some were easier to detect than others, especially if the perp placed it somewhere well out of reach. She stared with the rear of the vehicle, deciding that was the most logical place to put it.

It only took five minutes to find it. She stared at it for a long moment, then decided to leave it. She took a picture with Cole's phone and then returned to the front seat.

"This is it." She showed him the picture, which wasn't as clear as she'd have liked because of the darkness. "I left it there, though, so we can use it tomorrow."

He frowned. "Why would we want this guy to find us tonight?"

"He won't. We'll park this at a motel, then get a ride to a different one. Then we can pick up the rental SUV prior to the sting operation."

"The SUV will attract attention now that the rear window is broken," he said with a frown.

"We'll park it in the back, out of sight." She glanced at him with exasperation. "Why are you being so stubborn? We can make this work for us. I'm sure this guy will come after me tomorrow at our designated place. Between my phone and the rental car, he'll believe he has me cold."

"Yeah, that's exactly what I'm afraid of," Cole argued dully. "Cold as death."

She scowled. "I wish you had more faith in me and my team's skills."

"I have faith in God and in you and your tactical team." He pulled back out into traffic. "But that doesn't mean a plan can't go sideways."

"What's the alternative?" She tried to swallow her anger. "Seriously, Cole, what other option do we have? This perp knows far more about me than I do about him. We've tried to narrow down his identity from a list of possible suspects without success. I'm open to your thoughts on a better way to find him."

He was silent for a long minute. "I've spent these past five years as a Peabody detective tracking perps through solid police work. Digging into the victim's backgrounds, interviewing those closest to the vic, and going through forensic evidence. I feel like this idea of setting yourself up as bait is premature."

"I disagree. We've been playing defense for twenty-four hours without success. I'm ready to shake things up." He may as well accept the fact she wasn't changing her mind. "And as I said before, if you don't want to participate, that's fine. I'll get my teammates to provide backup."

"I'm in." He didn't sound happy about it, but that was too bad. "Where do you suggest we leave the SUV?"

"Good question." She tried to remember what other motels were in the area. Back in July, Roscoe had stayed in the Red Mill Motel. "Head west on the interstate. I know of a place that should work."

"I hope this guy doesn't do something crazy to hurt innocent people," Cole muttered.

"Me too. But keep in mind, he's already putting innocent people into harm's way by shooting at us. Not to mention setting Mr. Glen's house on fire."

"I know." He didn't look satisfied.

"Trust me, I don't want anyone hurt either. Which is exactly why we're going to set a trap for him tomorrow." She smiled grimly in using his own argument against him. "The sooner we get him behind bars, the safer everyone will be."

"I said I'd help." He sounded testy. "Where's this motel?"

She continued giving him directions to the Red Mill Motel. When they arrived, she was glad to see the red "No Vacancy" light was on. Having all the rooms full might give the perp pause since he wouldn't know which was their room.

Cole drove around to the far side of the motel, then backed the SUV into a narrow opening so the broken back window wasn't readily visible. Then they climbed out, grabbed their respective bags, and walked back out front.

"Call for a rideshare," she suggested.

"They may not have anyone nearby," he warned as he thumbed his phone screen.

"If not, I'll call someone on the team." Cassidy would likely volunteer to head out to pick them up.

"I found one." He sounded surprised. "Although it appears the quickest arrival time is fifteen minutes."

Fifteen minutes was a long time to stand around waiting outside the motel. Especially when the perp had put a tracker on their car. "Here's a better idea. Let's walk over to the restaurant to get a ride from there."

"Works for me." He pocketed his phone, and they quickly set out to cross the overpass of the interstate. It had only been two months ago that she'd helped rescue Roscoe's pregnant girlfriend, Libby, from a gunman determined to take her and her child out of the picture, permanently. Thankfully, they were able to catch the bad guys before anyone was hurt.

The way she hoped to get this perp in cuffs.

She kept an eye on the exit ramp leading to the Red Mill Motel, but not a single vehicle had headed that way. Thankfully, the rideshare driver showed up right on time.

"You're going to the Wildflower Motel?" the driver asked.

"Yes, please," Cole answered.

"I know the Red Mill is booked. There's a family reunion this upcoming weekend," the driver explained, clearly the chatty sort. She preferred those who drove in silence. "I've taken a few people into town to the local bar."

"That's nice." She managed a smile. "Do you know if the Wildflower has rooms?"

"Dunno," the guy said with a shrug. Then he caught her gaze in the rearview mirror. "Guess we'll find out when we get there."

She glanced at Cole, who surprised her by taking her hand. "Don't worry, sweetheart. We'll find a place to stay."

Sweetheart? Had he lost his mind? Then she realized he was playing a part for the driver. Which seemed a bit extreme, since she didn't see how the perp would know which rideshare they'd taken.

"I'm not worried, darling," she responded, giving his hand a warning squeeze. "I know we'll find something."

Their driver continued talking about the reunion and how nice it was to have more business in this rather remote area. She tuned him out, trying to think of a good place to use for their sting operation.

MPD had a safe house. She wasn't sure it was available, and it was located in a neighborhood that would make keeping eyes on the property from a distance more difficult. The home they chose needed to be somewhat remote while offering locations for her teammates to lie in wait.

That wasn't asking too much, was it?

At least she had her computer and could start looking for rental properties that would suit their needs.

They arrived at the Wildflower Motel fifteen minutes later, and the vacancy light was on. Well, part of it anyway, the middle letters were burned out.

"We appreciate your help," Cole said, releasing her hand to use his phone to pay and tip. "Have a good night."

"You too!" At least the guy was cheerful as he waved at them before taking off.

They headed inside to find a young adult sitting there, watching movies on her phone. She seemed annoyed to be interrupted. "I suppose you need a room?"

"Do you have two connecting rooms?" Cole asked.

"Nope. But I got a room with two beds, which is kinda the same thing." The girl eyed them curiously. "Want it or not?"

"We'll take it." Jina hadn't known Cole for long, but after spending the past twenty-four hours with him, she accepted that he was an honorable guy.

He used a credit card to pay. Since they'd used his phone to get there, she didn't complain. Her phone had likely been used as well as the tracker on the SUV. Without those two items in play, they should be safe.

"Room 5," the girl said, handing them a keycard. "Checkout time is ten a.m."

"Thanks," Cole murmured.

A few minutes later, they were in the room. She dropped her bag on the bed closest to the bathroom, sweeping the room with a critical eye. "Not the worst I've seen."

"You want first dibs on the bathroom?" Cole asked, stifling a yawn.

"Sure." She grabbed her overnight bag and ducked inside, reminding herself this was not the time to relive their kiss. Especially since she'd never shared a room with a man. Sure, she'd spent hours on a stakeout with her teammates in a car, but this felt different.

Her problem, not his. Cole had been married. He knew how to share personal space.

Splashing cold water on her face helped wash away her bone-weary fatigue. Her night of practically no sleep, combined with the various aches and pains from her work-out, followed by rolling the Jeep were catching up with her.

Emerging from the bathroom, she nodded at Cole. "Your turn."

As he disappeared inside, she pulled her laptop from her bag and began searching for rental properties. But all too soon, the words blurred on the screen. With a sigh, she set the computer aside and pulled the blanket up to her chin.

And despite her concerns about being stuck in a small space with Cole, she fell instantly to sleep.

COLE AWOKE to the scent of coffee. Blinking, he looked around until the small motel room came into focus.

Freshly showered and wearing clean clothes, Jina looked amazing. He still found it difficult to mesh the tough MMA fighter to the stunning beauty staring at the coffee maker as if willing it to hurry up and brew.

"Good morning." He swung out of bed and stretched. "Hope you slept okay."

"Surprisingly, I did." She glanced at him, then looked away. "I'm glad you're up. I found a couple of places that are worth checking out."

"Already?" He frowned, checking his watch. It was barely seven. "How long have you been up?"

"About an hour." She shrugged and reached for her coffee. "This thing only brews one cup at a time. Do you want one?"

"Sure." He leaned over to look at her computer screen as she filled the coffee maker with a fresh cup of water.

"It's not great coffee, but it will work in a pinch."

"I need a few minutes to shower and change." He grabbed his overnight bag and edged past her. "We need to discuss those locations you found before we call the rest of your team."

She arched a brow without saying anything. He sighed, knowing it wouldn't be easy to come up with some sort of compromise. As much as he understood and shared her frustration with the series of events, he wasn't sure that setting herself up at bait was the best solution.

Not that he had a better idea.

When he emerged from the bathroom, he found Jina back at her computer. She was right about the coffee, but he'd had worse, so he didn't hesitate to drink it. "Show me what you've found."

"Okay." She scooted off the bed and set the laptop on the small table. "I'm looking for a place that's far enough away from other homes yet isn't hours from here. Also a place that provides some coverage for the team."

"Sounds reasonable," he agreed.

"Yeah, well, there aren't a lot of options." She used the track pad to pull up the first property. "This is my top pick, although it's in Timberland Falls, and the cops there aren't big fans of ours."

Setting aside his coffee, he turned the screen to review the property details. Ignoring the interior of the home, which was probably what most renters would care about the most, he went through the outside photos. "I can see why you like it. The home sits on a full acre of land, and there are plenty of trees."

"Exactly." Her blue eyes gleamed with anticipation. "The only downside is that there are homes on either side. Not close, but not that far either."

"What about something near our current location?" he asked.

"I've looked at a few, but they have farmland surrounding them." She shrugged. "Too flat and open for what we need."

Her mention of farmland was a stark reminder of his cold case murder. He needed to give his lieutenant an update sometime today but wasn't sure how to broach the subject of Jina being a possible suspect.

Normally, he ran his cases by the book, but in this instance, he was tempted to keep Jina out of the case summary. At least for now.

Not that her involvement would be viewed in a positive light if he brought her into the conversation later. Just the opposite.

Lieutenant Karl Bell would yank him off the case before he could blink.

"There's one other place that might work," Jina said, oblivious to his internal struggle. She turned the computer back toward her and brought up the second image. "This one is in Surrey. There's a lot of construction going in on the other side of the nature preserve, which is why I bumped it down on the list."

He forced himself to concentrate on the screen. "I see what you mean. The weather is still nice enough that people could be walking through the nature preserve too."

"Hopefully not after dark, but yes, the new homes going in makes this one risky as far as innocent people being in danger." She grimaced. "I'll keep searching. I have a bad feeling the Timberland Falls PD won't be very understanding if there's another shootout involving MPD officers in their jurisdiction."

He frowned. "You make it sound like that happens on a regular occurrence."

"Yeah, well, it has happened at least three times in recent months."

"Really?" He eyed her warily. "Sounds like Zeke was right about you being a magnet for trouble."

"Not just me," she protested. "In fact, this is my first time in the spotlight."

He wasn't reassured by that. It seemed to him that Jina's job was more dangerous than his ever was. And not just because Milwaukee boasted a higher crime rate than Peabody—times ten—but because of her position on the team.

And the way Jina willingly put herself in harm's way.

Was this how Renee had felt about his job? He winced, regretting the way he'd downplayed her concerns.

He pushed the computer aside and turned to face her. "Promise me you won't be reckless about this."

She frowned. "I can't think of a time I've been reckless."

"Maybe not in recent months, but this guy is after you." He reached for her hand, and to his surprise, she didn't jerk away. "I think it's easier to think logically and rationally when others are in danger, compared to being the one sitting in the crosshairs."

To her credit, she didn't brush him off. Holding his gaze, she nodded. "You're right about that. I've had similar concerns back when my teammates were in danger. I don't have a death wish, Cole. I like my job, my life." Now her gaze slid from his, and her cheeks went pink. She tugged her hand from his, and for the first time ever, she appeared flustered. "I promise I won't be reckless."

"Good." He resisted the urge to pull her into a warm embrace. As far as his cold case murder was concerned, he was less than objective when it came to Jina.

Another hug and kiss would not help.

"I, uh, need to make some calls." She jumped to her feet, but he grabbed her hand to stop her.

"It's barely seven thirty. Not to mention, you can't use your phone." He couldn't help but smile at her frown. "How about we have breakfast first and call your teammates when we're finished. That way we can get some decent coffee."

"Okay." She crossed her arms over her chest. "That means we'll need another rideshare."

"Maybe." He reached for his phone. "Let's see if there's something within walking distance."

She nodded and moved to the window to peer outside. "It's overcast," she said with a frown. "I hope it doesn't rain on our parade."

"I don't think it's supposed to rain until later tonight." He used the map app and identified a chain breakfast restaurant a mile away. "Found one. Let's pack our stuff and get out of here."

Jina nodded and closed her laptop, tucking it into her overnight bag. She ducked into the bathroom to get her toiletries and stuffed them inside too. "Ready when you are."

She might look high maintenance, but he'd never met a more practical woman. The combination shouldn't have been attractive.

But there was no denying he liked her. Cared about her. And couldn't help but wonder if she'd see him again once this sting operation of hers was over.

In the three years since Renee's death, he'd never planned to become involved in another relationship. Especially not with someone as beautiful and prickly as Jina.

She wasn't his type. And she was a suspect in his cold case. Yet both of those deterrents didn't seem to matter.

"Cole?" She was frowning at him now. "Is something wrong?"

Yeah, I need my head examined, he thought with a sigh. But he shrugged and grabbed his bag. "Nope. I'm ready."

The overcast sky brought a distinct fall chill to the air. He'd stashed his sport coat in his bag and would have offered it to Jina if he'd thought she'd take it.

"I love fall," she said to his surprise. "It's my favorite time of year."

"What do you love the most?" He was curious to know everything about her, which should have sent more alarm bells screeching in his ear.

"The colors." She gestured to the trees. "They're only

just starting to turn, October is better, but I like the cooler weather, the colors, and football."

That made him laugh. "Of course, you like football."

She arched a brow. "Why not? My parents were big fans. It was one of the few things that helped me bond with my dad."

"Does Shelly like football too?"

"No, she's a girly girl. Shelly likes to cook and bake. I can't do either without burning the house down." Her smile faded. "I feel bad for Mr. Glen. Once this is over, I need to find out what I can do to help rebuild his duplex."

"You're a softie," he said with a grin.

"Yeah, well, don't tell anyone. I have a hard-core image to protect."

"Dully noted." He nodded toward the half-empty parking lot of the restaurant. "Looks like we won't have trouble getting a table."

"Good. I'm hungry." She frowned. "Although I don't know why, I didn't run my five miles this morning as usual."

"You make me feel like a sloth," he complained, opening the door for her.

They chose a booth in the back, and their server started them off with coffee. Jina held out her hand. "I need to borrow your phone to call Cassidy, Zeke, and Flynn."

He gave her the device and perused the menu. They didn't offer a full Irish like Rosie's Diner, but there were some options that should provide enough protein to get him through the day.

Sipping his coffee, he listened as Jina called her teammates, quickly explaining her need for a spare vehicle and her plan of setting herself up to draw in the shooter. Each time, she promised to call Rhy.

"Okay, they're all meeting us here for now." She slid the phone across the table.

He nodded at the phone. "Shouldn't you call Rhy?"

"After I have a plan, yes." She sat back as their server returned to take their orders. When that was finished, Jina leaned forward. "I know my boss well enough to know that he'll need time to inspect the plan for flaws."

"Okay." He could see her point and was glad Rhy would have to approve whatever scheme she and the others came up with. "How long before the rest get here?"

She shrugged. "Depends on traffic. They'll likely want to grab something to eat too."

"No problem." Their server to refill their cups. "We'll move to a bigger table."

Ten minutes later, their meals arrived. Jina clasped her hands in her lap, obviously waiting for him to say grace.

"Lord Jesus, we thank You for this food and for keeping us safe in Your care. Please continue to watch over us and to give us strength. Amen."

"Amen." She smiled. "I used to get annoyed when some of the guys said grace, but now that I've been targeted by this perp, I can see why some people lean on prayer."

"God is always there for you, Jina." He tried to keep his tone light. "Trust me."

"I do trust you." She looked thoughtful, then dug into her breakfast with gusto.

They were just finishing when his phone rang. Despite not recognizing the number, he answered. "This is Cole Roberts."

"It's Cassidy. I picked up a tail and may have compromised your location." She sounded calm despite the situation. "I'm driving past the restaurant, but I suggest you get Jina out of there."

How had Cassidy been followed? They'd left the tracker on his SUV! He tossed money onto the table and stood. "We need to go."

To her credit, Jina didn't argue. Rather than heading out the front, he boldly strode through the kitchen, ignoring the employees demanding they get out.

Maybe Jina's plan was the right move. Being forced to go on the run was getting old.

He wanted to nab this guy as much as she did.

CHAPTER ELEVEN

The rank scent of rotting garbage washed over them as they left the restaurant kitchen through the back door. Jina did her best to breathe through her mouth, despite the putrid odor emanating from a nearly overflowing dumpster. She eyed Cole. "What's going on?"

"Cassidy picked up a tail." Cole tugged her around the side of the dumpster. "She didn't take this exit. We're on our own until she or one of the others can get here."

She hadn't anticipated the shooter following one of her teammates. How would he even know about them? It wasn't as if they were out there on social media.

Although they had gotten some press in the recent months. Had he done a search on her? And then found a picture of her with her team?

Not good.

"Use your map app to find a rendezvous location." She hitched her bag higher on her shoulder and gestured to his phone. "Someplace close enough that we can get there on foot. Not the gas station across the street. Something farther away."

"There's not much around here aside from that gas station." His expression held doubt, but he did as she asked. It was all she could do not to snatch the phone away to look for herself.

"Okay, there's another gas station convenience store about a mile down the road."

"Still too close. What about heading in the opposite direction?" She huddled near him so she could look at the screen too. "He wouldn't expect us to cross the highway. We need a place that either Cass or one of the others can come back to meet us."

He manipulated the screen until he found another building. But there was no label associated with the structure. "What do you think? I'm not sure what this is."

"Maybe a restaurant or something else that went out of business. It's rather isolated, which I like. Two miles from here is good too. Take a screenshot and send it to Cassidy, Zeke, and Flynn."

While he did that, she moved away from the dumpster to the side of the restaurant that faced the highway. The early morning traffic was picking up, making it almost impossible to look for one black Honda, even without plates, as the cars were zooming past at well above posted speed limits.

Frustrating to be miles outside the city without a vehicle. She should have contacted Cass last night rather than letting her exhaustion overrule her common sense.

Hearing Cole's phone ring, she turned toward him. He showed her the display. Recognizing Zeke's number, she nodded and held out her hand.

"Zeke? Jina. Where are you? Cass was followed to this exit, so I need you to stay away for a while."

"How is that possible?" Zeke asked.

"Don't know. We'll swap theories later. Cole texted you a meeting point, but we need time to get there on foot. Say thirty minutes?"

"See you then." Zeke ended the call.

She handed Cole the phone. "There's not much coverage, so get ready to run."

"Got it." He pocketed the phone and hovered beside her at the side of the building. They waited until there was a break in traffic, then darted out. It wasn't easy to run with a bag slung over her shoulder, but she ignored the way it banged against her hip with every step. No way was she leaving her computer behind.

She ended up in the lead, and it was only when Cole stayed close behind her that she realized he was covering her six on purpose. She had to admit it was nice having another cop backing her up. One that had and would continue to put his life on the line for her.

The same way her teammates would. Yet there was something different about her relationship with Cole. More than typical teammate camaraderie.

A deeper connection she didn't have the time or inclination to name.

Upon reaching two large pine trees, she slowed her pace and ducked to use the evergreens as cover. Cole did the same. Moving more quietly now, she continued heading due south toward the building that had no name. Normally, she could run two miles without a problem. But not with a bag slung over her shoulder, and not when the goal was to stay out of sight.

This section of the road was relatively deserted. Whatever business had been housed in the seemingly empty building must have gone under a long time ago. Free map apps weren't always up to date.

"Car," Cole whispered.

She instantly dropped to the ground, spreading herself flat so to avoid being seen. Cole mirrored her movement beside her. Thankfully, their bags weren't that large and were easily hidden. The grass—well, mostly weeds—along this stretch of the road was long enough to provide some cover. Especially with the overcast sky hiding the sun.

But they weren't invisible. They needed to be prepared for the inevitable.

Easing her weapon from her holster, she found herself wishing, and not for the first time, that she had her sniper rifle with her.

Next time she was in trouble, she wasn't going anywhere without it.

If she survived long enough for a next time.

"White sedan," Cole murmured near her ear. "Probably not the shooter since Cassidy saw a black Honda."

She nodded while keeping her head down. By unspoken agreement, they waited for several long minutes after the sedan passed them before getting back up on their feet. A quick glance revealed that several round prickly burrs were stuck to her bag, clothing, and likely her hair. Hiding a grimace, she ignored the discomfort of the sharp pricks and focused on getting to their designated meeting point.

"We still have a mile and a half to go," Cole said as if reading her mind.

"Okay, let's pick up the pace." She broke into a jog, the bag once again slapping against her hip with every step. At this rate, they would be late for their meeting point, especially if they had to drop to the grass again for another car.

That meant covering as much ground as possible while the street was empty.

As before, Cole maintained his position behind her. Imagining the map of their location, she watched the opposite side of the road, hoping to spot the building before they came too close. Better to approach with caution. They'd assumed the structure was empty or abandoned but had no way of knowing for certain.

"Another car," Cole whispered. In unison, they dropped to the ground, hiding among the weeds, which were higher here. As much as she wanted to lift her head to look at the oncoming vehicle, she stayed down.

The car engine grew louder as it prepared to pass. Then the vehicle slowed, the engine dropping to a low idle.

Then the car engine went silent.

Her pulse kicked up. Maybe the shooter had spotted them. She almost hoped he had. Time to get rid of this guy once and for all.

Still holding her weapon, she slowly turned her head toward the road. Would she recognize the shooter? Or would he be a stranger? Her memory of the guys she'd taken on at the gym wasn't that clear. Once she'd proved her point, she'd mostly forgotten them.

Cole tensed beside her. Neither of them moved as they waited for the shooter to show.

There was nothing but a strained silence. Finally, she heard the swish of tall grass and weeds as the driver of the car stepped closer.

"Jina? Are you out there?" Hearing Zeke's voice made her relax. Lifting her head, she peered at her teammate.

"Yeah. We're here." She rose to her feet, holstered her weapon, then brushed at the prickly balls on her clothing as Cole did the same. She reached for her bag, scowling at her teammate. "Do you realize how close you came to being on the wrong end of my gun?"

"Oh, sorry." Zeke's grin was unrepentant. "You should be glad it's me, though. It was easy to see the depression of your bodies in the long grass. If the perp had driven by, he'd have spotted you from a mile away."

"Yeah, well, we didn't have much choice." She was irritated by his showing up like that, sending her blood pressure through the roof. "What was with the sneak attack anyway? Why didn't you just keep going? We agreed to meet at the abandoned building."

"Yeah, well, that's the thing." Zeke scratched the back of his neck. "The building is gone. It must have been bulldozed in the past few weeks; there are still ruts in the earth from a front loader."

Hearing that, it made sense that Zeke had come to find them. She sighed. "I didn't realize it had been destroyed. What about Cass and Flynn?"

"They're waiting at the site. I offered to come find you." Zeke gestured to a black SUV, not his truck, which had taken gunfire at the American Lodge, but likely another rental. She often wondered how much money Rhy paid in rental fees each year. Had to be more than what she paid for three months' rent. "I'll give you a ride."

"Thanks." She trudged toward the SUV, still picking burrs from her clothing. Cole was doing the same. Running a hand through her hair, she winced as she pulled several more burrs from the strands.

"I'll get them," Cole offered, pushing her hand out of the way.

"Climb inside the SUV first," Zeke advised, glancing behind them. "Cassidy lost the black Honda, but we still need to keep you hidden."

Resigned, she dropped her bag onto the floor, then climbed into the back seat. Cole slid in beside her, setting his bag down between his feet too. With the patience of a saint, he gently tugged burrs from her hair. She held herself still, keenly aware of his closeness. His fingers pulling burrs from her hair shouldn't have come across as intimate. Her ridiculous hormones were spiraling way out of control.

"You wouldn't have shot me, Jina," Zeke said. "You're too good of a cop for that."

"Don't bet on it." She held his gaze in the rearview mirror. "You should have announced yourself sooner. I truly thought you were the perp."

"She was seconds from jumping to her feet to confront you," Cole agreed, still pulling burrs from her hair. "And I would have joined her. Between the two of us, you wouldn't have stood a chance."

"I wish the shooter had found us." She winced when Cole tugged on a particularly tangled burr. "Then this mess would be over."

Zeke looked chagrined. "I hear you. I should have realized you'd be on edge. Next time I'll call out to you sooner." He gestured to an open area between some trees where two more vehicles were parked. "There's the rest of the cavalry."

"Just in time," Cole murmured. One last tug, then he turned away. "I think I got them all."

"Thanks." She sent him a sideways glance, then turned her attention to her waiting teammates. This wasn't the time to think about how much she wanted to kiss him again or how much she enjoyed hanging out with him. At least, when he wasn't looking at her as the primary suspect in his cold case.

Yeah, better to stay focused on the upcoming mission.

They had a lot to accomplish before dusk.

AS THEY GATHERED with the three members of her tactical team, Cole tried not to let his growing feelings for Jina show on his expression. From the way Zeke had narrowly eyeballed him in the rearview mirror, the feelings in question weren't much of a secret to anyone but possibly Jina herself.

Their close call with Zeke only pressed the point home. He'd been seconds away from throwing himself into the line of fire to protect her. He cared for her, more than he should. She was messing with his mind to the point he didn't even care if she had crushed Brad Crow's skull in. The more he learned about the guy, the more he was convinced the creep had gotten what he'd deserved. The way he'd stalked Jina, climbing into her bedroom, and also staring at the other pretty young women at the pub was not something to be taken lightly.

But uncovering Crow's killer wasn't his focus for today. Which only reminded him that he still needed to call his boss to provide an update on the case. He'd do that soon, but in truth, his sole mission was to keep Jina safe.

This so-called plan of hers better go off without a glitch or he was going to be royally ticked.

"The best option so far is to use the property in Timberland Falls," Jina said.

"Not Timberland Falls," Zeke groaned. "They hate us. I mean really, really hate us."

"Yeah, and I'm not sure how many more times they'll let us off with a warning," Cassidy added. The pretty redhead scowled. "Rhy had to work really hard to get us off the hook for that July shooting with Roscoe. I'm not sure he wants to face off with the Timberland Falls captain again."

"The second location isn't nearly as attractive," Jina said. "I'm sure Rhy would rather we have more coverage than worry about the Timberland Falls PD getting their undies in a bunch. Besides, if we do this right, no shots will need to be fired. Hence nothing for them to complain about."

"Famous last words," Flynn muttered.

Jina waved that off. "First, we need a place nearby to talk through some details. We found a GPS device on Cole's SUV and have reason to believe my phone is being tracked by this guy. That's why we needed a spare ride. Both the GPS and my phone will be useful in setting the trap, but we can't head out to the property yet. Not until we make sure it will suit our needs and that we can get Rhy on board."

"Where should we go?" Cassidy asked.

"How about that breakfast place? What was it?" Zeke frowned. "Oh yeah, the Pine Cone."

"Nope. That's too close to where we left my SUV," Cole interjected. "We should either head west or south."

"Hang on," Cassidy said, staring at her phone. "Okay, there's a chain restaurant four miles from here."

"I'm starving," Zeke announced. "Let's do it."

"Cole and I have eaten, but we can always drink more coffee," Jina said. "Which one of these cars is for us?"

"The rental." Zeke tossed the key fob high enough in the air for Jina to easily catch it. "I'll ride with Flynn to breakfast."

"Meet you there." He nodded to Cassidy and then followed Jina back to the SUV.

"Do you mind if I call my boss?" He glanced at her as he pulled his phone from his pocket.

"Go ahead." She frowned. "If you need me to drop you

off in Peabody so you can work, that's fine. I don't want you to risk losing your job."

If he was going to lose his job, it would be over his getting too close and personal with a suspect. "No need, I'll stick with you."

"If you're sure." She shrugged and pulled out into the road to follow Cassidy who was in the lead.

"Positive." He was hoping he might have time to do more computer work on the cold case if there was some downtime. Glancing at his watch, he realized it was going on nine in the morning. He'd hoped to simply leave a message, but hearing his boss's voice on the other end of the line proved that wasn't the case.

"Roberts, where have you been?" Lieutenant Bell demanded. "I thought you'd be here this morning."

"I had some car trouble." It wasn't exactly a lie, having the rear window shot out and finding a GPS tracker was troublesome. "But I'm happy to give you an update on the case."

"Oh, so you are working." Bell's tone dripped with sarcasm. "Let's hear it."

He took a moment to gather his thoughts. "We'll start with the ME's report. He provided an ID on our victim. Young adult male with a dental match to Bradley Crow. As you know, Crow was reported missing roughly twelve years ago. He was twenty years old at the time of his going missing, and I suspect he was killed shortly after his disappearance."

"That's a good start," Bell said with reluctant approval.

"Yes, sir. I interviewed his parents yesterday. They weren't as forthcoming as I would have liked. Obviously, I read the report from the previous detective, since retired, prior to our meeting and tried to ask questions that might capture them in a lie. But they stuck to their same story."

"And what story is that?"

"Per the detective's notations, they didn't report their son missing until three months after the fact, which in and of itself is suspicious. When I pressed them about why they'd waited so long, they informed me that Brad was an adult and could make his own decisions. Which is true, but not normal parent behavior on their part. I'd think most parents would be concerned if their twenty-year-old son dropped off the grid, especially in this day of cell phones. Apparently, they assumed he was either staying with a friend or had moved to Madison to find work. When I asked specifically about why Brad would head to Madison, they admitted he didn't know anyone living there. I can't help but wonder why they chose to believe he'd headed to Madison rather than Milwaukee or one of the other suburbs."

"Is that why you don't believe them? You think they made up the move to Madison to cover up their role in his disappearance?"

"Possibly," Cole admitted. "I think Brad's father is holding back. I sensed a strange vibe from him when it came to discussing his son. The old man owned and ran Peabody's Pub. Brad dropped out of high school to work for them, but apparently, Henry Crow didn't think much of his son's work ethic. Brad allegedly made it clear he thought his being the owners' son meant he should take over as bar manager, but the old man flat-out said that wouldn't happen. Brad's mom reluctantly confirmed they argued over that point the very last time they saw him alive."

"You think they were in a physical fight?" Lieutenant

Bell asked. "Maybe the kid fell and hit his head by accident."

"Not sure about that, the old man doesn't come across as being in good shape. I'd have to think the younger Crow would have the advantage in a physical scuffle. But as you know, anything is possible, his dad could have been in better shape twelve years ago. I also went to Peabody's Pub to speak with Ian Muller, the former bar manager and current bar owner."

"Wait, the Crows don't own it anymore?"

"Nope, they sold it about eighteen months ago to Ian and Amy Muller. Ian remembers Brad very well. Claims the kid showed up late for his shifts or didn't bother coming in at all. He also confirmed that Henry Crow assured him that Brad was no threat to his bar manager job. In fact, everything I heard from Muller echoed what the parents said." He hesitated, then added, "Muller mentioned there was one time that Brad got in trouble with a bar patron. Seems Brad stared at one of the young daughters with such intensity he made the girl uncomfortable. The girl's father stormed over to give Brad a piece of his mind and warned him about leaving his daughter alone."

"Yeah, well, that's interesting, but I don't think it's pertinent to the case. It's a pretty weak motive," Bell said. "It's not like the vic touched the girl or made an obscene gesture. Can't imagine why some father would bash his head in, then hide the body to cover it up."

"True, but my thought was that Brad could have followed them home or maybe ran into them again at some other time." Even as he made the statement, he realized that wasn't likely. "Either way, Ian Muller doesn't remember their names. He claims they weren't locals, so I can't exactly follow up on the incident."

"Hmm." The progress he'd made on the case, minimal as it was, seemed to smooth Bell's annoyance. "What's your next step?"

"Um . . ." He had to think for a moment. "The parents gave me the name of Wade Adams. He was Brad's friend at the time. I plan to track him down and interview him next."

"Okay, but what if Wade doesn't give you anything useful?" His boss was awfully persistent this morning. "What's next?"

Somehow, he managed to avoid looking at Jina. She was the biggest clue yet, but he had purposefully kept her out of his report. He cleared his throat. "I'm sure Wade knows more of Brad's friends. Sounds like the parents were busy with the bar and didn't pay much attention to what their son did in his downtime. I was also thinking I'd find and interview some of Brad's female classmates. If he paid an inordinate amount of attention to young women, maybe one of them can shed some light on who might want him dead."

"Hrmph." Bell grunted, then said, "Fine, but work fast and keep me informed. We've managed to keep the name of the dead body found in the new construction zone out of the news, but I don't think that will last long. Especially now that you've interviewed his parents and that Muller guy. Word is going to leak out very soon. That could be a good or a bad thing."

"I understand." He understood how this sort of news worked. People would call and claim they saw something suspicious, even if they didn't. He also knew that Lieutenant Bell's definition of working fast did not include taking a day off to set up Jina's sting operation. "I'll follow up with you later."

"Not too late. I want results, Roberts." With that, his boss ended the call.

Jina had obviously heard his part of the conversation. She slowed the rental to pull into the restaurant parking lot. Sliding the gearshift into park, she glanced over at him. "You didn't mention me."

"No." He held her gaze, then shrugged. "I may have to at some point."

She nodded thoughtfully. "I appreciate you giving me the benefit of doubt."

He was giving her more than that. He was putting his entire career on the line for her. "I believe you didn't kill him. I just need to figure out who did."

Her eyes widened, then her expression softened. "Thanks for your support."

Support? He'd call it more like going out on a very long, skinny, and about-to-snap tree limb for her. "Yeah, well, don't forget you promised to help me solve this thing once we identify your shooter."

"Gladly." She killed the engine and was about to open her door when she paused, then turned to face him again. "Cole?"

"Yeah?"

She leaned toward him just as Zeke rapped sharply on the window. "Hey, hurry up. I'm hungry."

"Never mind. We'll talk later." She turned away and pushed open her door. He wanted to hang onto the moment, but there was no point in wishing for a private moment with her teammates watching.

She took a moment to grab her bag from the back seat. He decided to grab his, too, in case they needed two computers, then quickly joined her.

Catching her hand, he said, "I'd like to talk later." Since Zeke was already crossing the threshold with the others, he risked brushing a kiss across her cheek.

She blushed, then gently squeezed his hand before tugging it free.

The brief caress shouldn't have made his pulse spike, but it did. And as he followed her to the round table the others had begun to gather at, he silently vowed to protect her.

No matter what the day might bring.

CHAPTER TWELVE

It was official. Jina had completely lost her mind and had little hope of finding it again. Doing her best to ignore Cole who sat next to her at the round table in the restaurant dining room, she pulled her laptop from her bag and set it on the table. To her surprise, Cole did the same with his computer.

It made sense for them to work, as they'd already eaten. When their server arrived, she gladly accepted more coffee. Jina had a feeling she was going to need the extra caffeine.

Cassidy, seated to her left, leaned forward to see the screen. "Is that the place in Timberland Falls?"

"Yes." She didn't expound on that, as their server had returned to fill their coffee cups and to take their orders. Once Zeke, Flynn, and Cassidy had finished, she turned the computer more fully. "Okay, here's the first location I found."

Cassidy took the computer, clicked through the screen to see the property photos, then passed the laptop to Zeke. After he finished, he handed it to Flynn.

"I like it because the house is far enough from the neighbors with several trees and bushes to provide protection." She glanced at Cole, who was working on his laptop. "Are you looking for an alternative location?"

"Just checking something." After a long moment, he nodded thoughtfully. "This property is roughly two miles from the apartment building where Oliver Norman and his buddy Evan Wilde live."

She frowned. "I don't understand why that matters."

He shrugged, glancing at the confused expressions on her teammates' faces. "We never made it over there to interview them. Might be worth a stop along the way."

She swallowed a sigh. "Oliver and Evan belong to Mike's MMA gym, the location of the first shooting attempt. Oliver tried to hit on me, so I invited him to a sparring match. I put him down on the mat, which may have embarrassed him."

Zeke grinned. "He had no clue what he was getting into, huh?"

She couldn't help but smile back. "He did not. And while I probably struck a blow to his ego, I don't see him as a suspect in these attacks. Not just because being embarrassed is a weak motive, but he and his buddy Evan are two peas in a pod. They seem to go everywhere together, one egging the other on. The perp coming after me is a loner. If Ollie was a part of this, he'd be coordinating attacks with Evan."

"I agree in theory with your assessment of our perp, but it's always helpful to speak personally with suspects." Cole was sticking to his point. "Preconceived perceptions can be wrong."

She glanced at him, wondering if he was talking about her or Oliver and Evan. Either way, he was right. In many of the situations her teammates had gotten into over the past eight months, they'd been wrong about who they believed to be their primary suspect in a case more times than she cared to admit.

"Can't hurt to talk to them," Flynn said, "since we'll be in the neighborhood."

"Maybe." She thought interviewing Ollie and Evan would be a waste of time but decided to move on. "For now, let's focus on getting the location nailed down, then decide how to draw the shooter out." She had to stop again because their server returned with more coffee.

"Your breakfasts will be ready shortly," she said with a special smile toward Zeke.

"Thank you." Zeke smiled, and their server blushed.

She fought the urge to roll her eyes. "Flirt on your own time, Zeke."

"This isn't my own time?" Zeke pretended to look confused. "I don't think we're being paid by the MPD for this little extravaganza."

Normally, she didn't mind bantering with the team, but not today. She gave him a narrow glare. "Focus. Unless anyone has a better idea, I'm going to book this place while it's still available."

"Go for it," Cassidy agreed.

She booked the rental using her own credit card information. Hard to imagine the shooter would have the ability to track her credit card payments, but if he did, it played well with her scheme. She planned to use the GPS tracked rental and her phone as a beacon.

Hopefully, both items would scream, *Come and get me*.

"One thing to consider is that this guy could try to take you out while you're en route to the property," Cole said. "Considering we left the SUV out at the Red Mill Motel, the moment you get in the vehicle and start driving toward

Timberland Falls, the perp will know exactly where you are."

She nodded thoughtfully. "Maybe I drive the SUV to the precinct first. I'm sure he'll hold off trying to intercept me until after I leave the police station."

"It's still several miles from the precinct to Timberland Falls," Flynn pointed out.

"I understand the risk." She looked at each of her team-mates, then at Cole. "I doubt he'll make a move in broad daylight. There's no need to do that, especially when he finds the SUV has stopped at a rental property."

Despite Cole's clear dissatisfaction with her idea, he nodded in agreement. "I agree he's more likely to shoot during dusk. His few daylight attempts haven't gone well."

"Okay, that means the rest of us have to get into position before you show up," Zeke said. "What time do you plan to make the trip to the precinct, then again to Timberland Falls?"

She thought about that for a moment. "The later in the afternoon, the better. I don't want you guys to have to stay in place for hours."

"I'd like to ride with you," Cole said.

She grimaced and shook her head. "Better if I go alone. If he does follow me, I want him to think I'm vulnerable."

"No one who knows you would ever think that," Flynn protested. "I doubt this guy is an idiot."

"Maybe not an idiot, but stupid enough to keep coming after me." She found it difficult to imagine anyone harboring that deep of a grudge against her.

"I can hide in the back seat. He'll never see me." Cole reached for her computer. After a moment, he smiled with satisfaction. "Just as I thought. This place has an attached garage. I can hide inside with you without this guy knowing."

She wanted to protest that the added protection wasn't necessary, but Cassidy jumped in. "Good idea, Cole. I'm sure Rhy will like knowing you have support inside the house."

When Zeke and Flynn nodded, she gave up. "Okay, fine. What else do we need?"

Their server arrived with three breakfast meals. She refilled their coffee again, lingering over Zeke's cup, before moving on to her next table.

"What do we need other than Rhy's blessing?" Flynn looked thoughtful. "We can cover the outside of the property well enough. But how do you want us to take this guy down? Are you anticipating he'll drive up to the house or try to sneak in?"

It was a good question. She glanced at Cole, who shrugged. "If he believes I'm in there alone, I think he'll try to sneak up to the place in the dark. I'll be counting on one of you to grab him." It bothered her to think she wouldn't be the one to take the perp down. She glanced at Cassidy. "Unless you want to swap places with me."

"No, I'll stay outside." Cassidy arched a brow. "If this guy has binocs, he'll notice we don't look anything alike."

"Yeah, okay. I'll take the house." She sipped her coffee, trying to come up with another way to safeguard her team. "We may need one more person to cover the outside."

"I'll contact Steele," Zeke offered as he chomped on a slice of bacon. "He was glad to help us stake out the strip mall."

"I can do that, you're eating." She reached for her phone, only to remember she had it turned off. Cole noticed and slid his over to her. She picked it up. "And if he's busy, we can try Brock or Raelyn."

"Raelyn and Isaiah are out of town for a belated honeymoon," Cassidy said. "But Grayson should be around."

Thankfully, Steele answered on the first ring. "Delaney."

"It's Jina, using Cole's phone. Are you busy today? I need help."

"I can be there in twenty," her teammate answered without hesitation. "But I need to ask if Rhy knows about this. He wasn't too happy to be out of the loop regarding the incident at the American Lodge."

"He's my next call." She quickly filled him in. "Stay where you are for now, we'll let you know when it's time to move."

"Sounds good. I'll be waiting."

As all eyes were on her, she ended that call and tapped Rhy's number on the screen. He didn't answer, so she left a quick message.

"I'm sure Rhy will call back soon." Noticing her three teammates were just about finished with their meals, she added, "Maybe we should reconvene at the precinct. It's too early to head out to Timberland Falls."

The others nodded. "I like that plan," Zeke announced. "We need to gear up anyway." He narrowed his gaze on Jina. "As the target, you need to be well protected."

"I will be. I have all of you, don't I?" Zeke's comment reminded her of her sniper's rifle that was still sitting in her upper-level apartment. Swinging by the duplex wouldn't take too long, but she couldn't be sure that she'd be allowed inside. Probably not a priority since her plan didn't require the weapon. For one thing, she'd be inside the house waiting for him to show. And if he did manage to sneak past the others, he'd be too close for her to use the long gun.

She was better with the rifle than her handgun, but she was confident she could take him down with her service weapon if needed.

When Cole's phone rang, he simply passed it to her. Recognizing Rhy's number on the screen, she quickly answered. "Hey, Rhy. Got my message?"

"Yeah. Walk me through it."

She did so, keeping her voice low so the conversation couldn't be heard beyond their table. When she finished, there was a long silence.

"What's wrong? Did I forget something?" She hoped he wasn't backing out of supporting her to do this.

"No, I'm just thinking. I like the idea of you guys stopping here for a while. I'll have Gabe work on getting a blueprint of the property. Sounds like there's some coverage, but it's not like being out in the middle of the woods."

"True. I didn't want to go out too far, or he'd suspect a trap." She nodded to the others as she spoke to let them know Rhy was on board. "Have Gabe get all the intel he can. We'll be there in an hour or less."

"See you then." Rhy ended the call.

"We're a go." She handed Cole his phone back. "I only wish we didn't have to wait until dark. Sitting around doing nothing is going to drive me crazy."

"It will drive all of us crazy," Flynn agreed. "But waiting for darkness to fall is better."

The pretty server came back with their check. She placed a hand on Zeke's back as she set it down beside him. "Do you need anything else?"

"No, we're good," Flynn said with a wry smile. The pretty server barely glanced at him. "Thanks anyway."

"I hope you come back to dine with us again soon." She finally moved away.

"Sheesh, Zeke, what is up with that?" Cassidy groused. "I thought Grayson was the chick magnet."

"He's taken." Zeke grinned, then pulled cash from his pocket to pay the bill. "Ready to hit the road?"

"Yep." Jina closed her laptop and tucked it into her bag. "I'll take a rideshare to the Red Mill Motel to pick up the SUV, then meet you at the precinct."

"I'm going with you," Cole said firmly. He'd shut his computer too.

Swallowing her argument, she simply stood and slung her bag over her shoulder. Then on second thought, she handed it to Cassidy. "Would you mind taking this with you?"

"Not at all." Cassidy took the bag. Cole must have decided to go along with that idea, as he handed his to Flynn before coming over to stand at her side.

"Ready?" he asked.

"Of course." Apparently, Cole was determined to be her shadow, whether she liked it or not.

The biggest problem? She liked it.

More than she should.

FOLLOWING JINA OUTSIDE, Cole wished he could poke more holes in her plan. The time frame of not heading out to the rental until late afternoon was a bit of a problem.

He was torn between wanting to find and interview Brad Crow's friend Wade Adams and sticking close to Jina. His boss expected him to make some progress on the cold case murder investigation, but the last time he'd left her alone to interview Brad's parents, she'd nearly been killed.

Nope, leaving her wasn't an option. He probably wouldn't be able to concentrate on the interview anyway as he'd be too preoccupied on what she was doing. In the past twenty-four hours, he couldn't shake the feeling that he needed to stay close.

At least until they had this guy in handcuffs.

While Jina and her teammates had discussed the details of the upcoming operation during breakfast, he'd begun searching for Wade Adams. Finding an old online Peabody High School yearbook for Wade's senior year had helped. He'd actually taken the time to look at Jina's yearbook picture too. She had been beautiful back then, but she was even more stunning now.

No surprise that Brad had become fixated on her. He really needed to interview some of the guy's female classmates. He doubted Jina had been the first girl he'd watched from afar.

But she may have been the last.

Shaking that dire thought off, he'd focused on examining the younger version of Brad's buddy, trying to use facial feature markers that would stay the same over time. Even so, spotting someone who looked like Wade Adams on social media was slow going. He wasn't a facial recognition expert and had thought they may need technical help when he'd finally landed on a possible match.

And if that guy he'd found on social media was the correct Wade Adams, he currently lived and worked as a construction worker in Peabody.

Interesting that Adams could be involved in the same construction project where Brad Crow's body had been uncovered.

It was a key connection that needed to be explored.

But not today. Pushing his day job concerns aside, he used his phone to find a rideshare. "Looks like we have a ten-minute wait."

"Takes longer to get a ride this far outside of the city," she mused.

He shrugged. "At least we have the option of getting around without a vehicle."

"Yeah." She sighed. "I miss my Jeep."

"I know." He watched the dot on the screen as their ride approached. "We're looking for a white four-door sedan."

She nodded, not paying any attention to her teammates heading out without them. "I really hope this guy shows at the rental in Timberland Falls." She glanced at him. "I want this over and done with."

"Me too." On that, they could agree. "When will you turn your phone on?"

She thought about that. "I think I should wait until we get to the precinct. This guy may be wondering why it's off, and it will appear as if I ran out of battery and had to wait until we got someplace where I could borrow a charger."

"Smart move." The dot on his screen was growing closer. "That's our ride up ahead."

They watched the white sedan pull up. After comparing the guy's face to the one on his phone, he opened the back door for Jina.

"Red Mill Motel?" the driver asked.

"Yes, but if you could let us out a mile to the north of the motel, that would be great," Jina said. "Get off the interstate but keep going past the place. I'll let you know when to drop us off."

The guy looked confused by that but shrugged and pulled away from the breakfast restaurant.

"You think the perp is watching the motel?" he asked in a low voice.

"I doubt it. He has no reason to hang out there with the GPS tracker on the vehicle." She grimaced. "I just think it's better to take precautions. We need to check if the GPS is still there. Or if anything else has been tampered with."

"Agree." He tried to relax, but it wasn't easy. He figured relaxing wouldn't happen until they had this perp behind bars.

The trip to the Red Mill Motel didn't take too long. As requested, the driver went past the establishment without stopping.

"This is good," Jina said. "Thanks."

"Whatever you say." The driver eyed them curiously in the rearview mirror but wisely chose not to ask anything further.

Cole added a generous tip before sliding out of the car. He was glad he and Jina had given their bags over to her teammates. Sneaking up on the motel in broad daylight would be difficult enough without the added bulkiness.

The sky overhead was still overcast, but not nearly dark enough to hide their approach. In silent agreement, they moved away from the side of the road toward the ridge of trees.

"Let's split up to approach the place," Jina said. "We can cover more ground that way."

He didn't like it but reluctantly nodded. "Fine. Give me a few minutes to head around to the back side of the trees."

"Okay." She knelt on the ground behind a large bush. "I don't have a phone, so I'll give you three minutes, then will continue moving forward."

"Hold on." He reached for her hand.

"What?" She looked impatient.

"Take my phone." He pulled the device from his pocket, put it on silent, then handed it over to her. "I should have thought of this before, but my watch is linked to my phone. We can call or text if we run into trouble."

She smiled, making him realize he'd do just about anything to make her happy. She gratefully accepted it. "Good idea. Thanks."

"Anytime." Stifling the urge to kiss her, he forced himself to move away, easing through the brush. He was in over his head with Jina and, not for the first time, found himself praying he wasn't making a mistake in judgment.

After about ten yards, he turned, walking at an angle that should take him to the back side of the motel. Not too far, hopefully, from the spot where they'd left the rental SUV.

And the GPS tracker.

The trees provided some cover, but he still felt exposed. The only good thing about this location was that there weren't private residences nearby. In the distance, he could see the inevitable gas station that seemed to be on every interstate exit known to man, but otherwise, he didn't see anyone nearby.

Yet there was still the chance someone would come upon them and decide to call the local police to report something suspicious.

It took a solid ten minutes for him to get into a position where he could see the SUV through the trees. It was up against the back side of the building, but that meant there were three sides that could have been tampered with.

He paused and scanned the area for a moment. Seeing nothing suspicious, he slowly edged closer, knowing Jina would be approaching from his left.

She had more coverage, which was a good thing.

When he was within ten yards of the vehicle, he caught the pungent odor of gasoline. He froze, immediately thinking of the turpentine that the perp used to start the fire in Mr. Glen's duplex. Mitch Callahan had said the perp had used it as fuel to start the fire.

Were they facing a similar situation here?

He wasn't sure what to make of the gasoline smell, but it was not good. Lifting his arm to see his watch, he quickly found the text app. It was painstaking to use the small screen, but he managed to send a text. *Smell gas.*

It seemed to take an inordinate length of time for her to respond. *Me 2. The perp?*

Good question. The strong odor of gasoline could be because someone tried to siphon his tank. With gas prices on the rise, there had been more cases reported of gas theft.

Or it could be that the vehicle was wired to blow.

He carefully typed a response on the mini screen. *I'll check. Cover me.*

Her reply was quicker this time. *Will do.*

Satisfied, he edged closer to the SUV. As he did so, the gasoline fumes grew stronger. He still had the key fob in his pocket, and the thought of the car blowing up at the click of the button gave him pause.

Could this perp be smart enough to have made and planted a bomb? If so, why the intense gasoline smell?

He didn't like it but continued easing closer. Without his phone, it wouldn't be easy to see beneath the vehicle. But that didn't stop him.

Seeing motion to the left, he froze, then scowled when Jina emerged. She held up the phone without saying anything, as if reading his mind about how he'd need the light.

They were both close enough to the vehicle to know the

shooter wasn't in the immediate area. There had been no sign that anyone had come through the woods in the same place he had either. Plus, they'd stayed low enough that anyone watching from afar through a scope or binocs wouldn't have spotted them.

He hoped.

He held out his hand for the phone, then stretched out on the ground. Flicking the flashlight app on, he aimed the beam beneath the vehicle's frame.

To his shocked surprise, it only took him a few minutes to find what he was looking for. A crude pipe bomb that was located near the fuel tank. Sweeping the beam of light over the ground, he saw the gasoline spill had killed several weeds on the ground.

Explosives were not his area of expertise, but he surmised the idea was that they'd start the car, the bomb would blow, and the extra gasoline would make sure they went up in a ball of flames.

He turned to glance toward Jina. He mouthed the word *bomb,* then began to edge away from the car.

Silently praying the explosive device wasn't on a timer or, worse, could be triggered to blow from afar.

CHAPTER THIRTEEN

The perp had planted a bomb? Jina's mind immediately went into problem-solving mode. They had to evacuate the motel, then get her team to head out and defuse the device.

She performed a quick scan of the area as Cole inched his way toward her. There was no sign of the perp, but that wasn't very reassuring. She hated to admit that she hadn't anticipated a bomb.

Using his phone, she called Cass and got straight to the point. "We need you guys at the Red Mill Motel ASAP. Explosive device found beneath the rental SUV."

"We're on the way," Cass said without hesitation. "And we'll call the locals too."

"Thanks, we'll take care of things here." She was about to give Cole his phone back, then changed her mind. She might need the light. "Backup is on the way. I need you to evacuate the motel."

"What are you doing?" he asked with a frown.

"I'm going to take a closer look at that device. I may be able to neutralize it." As she moved past him, he grabbed her hand.

"Have you lost your mind?" Stark fear darkened his eyes. "What do you know about defusing bombs?"

Not as much as Rhy or Grayson, their tactical team explosives experts. Yet there was no point in focusing on her weakness. "I've had some training. Now please get those people out of the building."

He shook his head as if he wanted to argue. Then he released her hand. "Stay safe," he murmured.

"You too." She resisted the urge to kiss him. After Cole rose to his feet and headed to the motel lobby to get everyone out, she gingerly moved closer to the rental car.

She slowed her breathing, forcing her pulse to settle much the way she did before taking a long-distance shot. The horrible gasoline smell made her stomach twist. Ignoring it as best she could, Jina used Cole's phone flashlight app to see what they were up against.

The device was near the rear wheel and far too close to the gas tank. As she examined the bomb more closely, she quickly realized it was a basic pipe bomb. There was no timer that she could see or a trigger that could be detonated from a distance.

Thankfully, whoever this perp was hadn't gotten too creative. She was confident she could safely remove it.

Unless there was a hidden surprise she couldn't see from this angle.

Don't borrow trouble, she silently lectured herself. Rolling onto her back, she wiggled farther beneath the SUV. There was barely enough clearance for her to maneuver without using the jack to raise it up, which made her realize that neither Grayson nor Rhy would be able to access this thing.

In the distance, she heard voices as Cole worked to get the motel guests and employees evacuated. Then car engines started, as patrons decided to get out of there. She didn't blame them for wanting to distance themselves from a possible explosion.

That wasn't an option for her.

Doing her best in the cramped space, she examined the duct tape keeping the pipe bombs wrapped together and to the undercarriage. Digging the penknife from her pocket— the guys always carried them, so she decided to do the same —she carefully sawed back and forth with the blade, slicing through the wide tape. When she realized she was holding her breath, she took a moment to breathe normally again.

Panic was not her friend.

It wasn't easy to work in the confined space with the three pipe bomb explosives bound together looming less than an inch from the tip of her nose. But now that she was seeing it closer, she felt more confident in her ability to remove them without blowing herself up.

Always better to think positive.

The first bit of duct tape gave way, leaving one more on the other side. She had to jiggle her position around to see better, then continued with her task. If God really was watching over her, she hoped He would keep her safe long enough to protect the others.

The thought brought another strange sense of calm washing over her. She had this, no problem. Without fear, she sawed through the last portion of tape, then slowly moved the device from the undercarriage. With the pipe bombs cradled in one hand, she stretched out her arm intending to set the bomb down, then hesitated.

Maybe placing the bomb on the gasoline-soaked ground wasn't the smartest idea.

Keeping the bomb in one hand, she used her free hand and the heels of her feet to inch out from beneath the car.

Her movements were awkward, her shirt riding up her back with each motion. The entire process seemed to be taking longer than it had to crawl in.

The wail of police sirens was a welcome indication that local law enforcement personnel would be there shortly. And the voices from the front of motel had quieted, making her believe Cole had managed to get them all safely out of the building.

"Jina? What can I do to help?"

Angling her head, she saw Cole hunched beside her. "Grab my feet and pull me the rest of the way out. But gently," she cautioned, "I have the bomb in my hand."

"Your hand?" He sounded horrified as his strong hands wrapped around her ankles. He drew her the rest of the way out from beneath the car.

Still holding the bomb with one hand, she levered up into a sitting position. "Thanks."

"What are you going to do with it?" He gestured toward the device.

Good question. She wasn't keen on holding it indefinitely. As she glanced around, she spied the dumpster. "See if there's a box in there."

Cole hurried over to peer inside, then reached inside. He pulled out a small box. "Will this work?"

"Yes." She stood and closed the gap between them. While he held the box, she carefully placed the device inside. "Now I need this to go back inside the dumpster until the bomb squad arrives."

"I can do that." He was taller and had a longer reach, so she didn't argue. Oddly, she was more nervous for him than she had been for herself. He lifted the box, then reached over the rim of the dumpster to set it down.

"Okay, thanks. The sides of the dumpster should help

minimize the damage if it goes off for some reason." She grabbed Cole's hand. "Let's get away from here."

He looked relieved by that suggestion.

They hurried around to the front of the motel. Two squads were taking the interstate exit to the motel. Several room doors hung open, and in some cases, half-packed suitcases were still lying open on the beds.

Pulling her badge from her pocket, she headed over to meet the responding officers. "MPD Officer Jina Wheeler, I have removed the explosive device and set it in the dumpster behind the building."

"You removed it?" The first officer was a portly guy old enough to be her father. "By yourself?"

The constant sexist comments never failed to annoy her. Would he have acted so outraged if Cole had done the deed? Doubtful. She swallowed her ire. "Yes. I'm with the tactical team and have some IED training."

"I'm Peabody Detective Cole Roberts." Cole flashed his badge as well. "I've evacuated the motel, but you may want to close the exit so no one else drives past the place until the device has been removed from the area."

The officers exchanged a look, then the portly one nodded at the younger guy. "Let's go ahead and close both exits."

"I have my teammates coming too," Jina added. "I'm hoping they'll bring the IED disposal van with them."

"We'll let them through when they arrive." The portly guy eyed her with a new respect. "Nice work."

She nodded, then waved him off.

"I don't know how you managed not to punch him in the nose," Cole muttered.

Despite the grim situation, that made her laugh. "It's

not easy." Her expression turned somber. "Where do you think the perp is hiding?"

Cole sighed. "I don't know. I have a feeling he didn't want to be too close in case the device did go off. It was close to the brake pads where the friction could have ignited it when we were driving. And it was so close to the gas tank, the entire rear of the SUV would have blown."

"I saw that." She didn't know a lot about car engines but had assumed the decision to locate the device near the rear wheels and the gas tank had been intentional. "I really want to find this guy."

"Me too." He glanced at her. "I'm not sure he's going to fall into your trap, though. The way he targeted the rental SUV makes me think he knew we'd left it here on purpose to throw him off. And his response was to plant the bomb."

She shared his concern. There was no doubt in her mind this guy was taunting her. Reveling in the way he'd been able to stay one step ahead of them. "I know, but what other option do we have? It's worth a try."

"I still don't like it."

He didn't have to like it as long as he went along with the plan. She was about to say something more when she caught sight of Cassidy leaning out her driver's side window to speak with the officer blocking the exit.

Cassidy and Flynn arrived first, followed by Zeke, and then Grayson who accompanied Gully Sullivan and his black van, which housed Dottie, their robot.

When they were all assembled outside the motel lobby, she filled them in. When she finished, Grayson eyed her with admiration. "Well done. If you weren't such an ace sniper, we could do more IED training with you."

"I'd rather be a sniper," she said. "But the device is in a

box sitting in the dumpster. It was the only place I could think of to minimize the damage."

"That's exactly what I would have done." Grayson turned to Gully. "Grab the bomb box from the back of the van. I don't think we need Dottie for this."

Gully obliged. She followed Grayson to the dumpster, watching as he reached in, grabbed the bomb, then carefully set it in the heavy-duty bomb box. Once the device was secure, she breathed easier.

"What's with the gasoline scent?" Grayson asked as he carried the box back to the van.

"Honestly, I'm not sure." She glanced around the area in question before following Grayson back to Gully's van. "My only thought was that our perp splashed the gasoline around to help deliver a bigger explosion."

"He's a real jack of all trades, huh?" Grayson set the box in the van, then stepped back to close the steel reinforced doors. There was no denying an acute sense of relief in knowing the device was no longer a threat. "Shooting, arson, and now setting an IED."

"Yeah. It only reinforces my theory that this guy has a background in law enforcement." She glanced over as Cole joined them. "Despite this latest bomb threat, I still think heading out to the Timberland Falls rental tonight is our best chance to draw him into the open."

"I doubt he'll show," Cole said bluntly. "But I'll go along with the rest of you on this."

"Cole has a point," Grayson said as the others clustered around. "Maybe we should think about where this all started?"

She frowned. "You mean at Mike's MMA gym?"

Grayson shrugged. "Just a thought. It's relatively

isolated. And you had planned to stake out the strip mall behind it."

She mulled that over for a moment, then shook her head. "I don't think this guy will show up there."

"Why not?" Cole asked. "He knows you go to the gym on a regular basis."

"True." She sighed. Thinking like a killer wasn't easy. If she had some sort of clue as to who this guy was, it would help. "Let's head back to the precinct and talk it through. I'm not sure which way to go on this."

"Do you think it's safe to take the rental?" Cole asked.

"No, we should leave it here." She wasn't sure why, but she felt strongly they needed a different vehicle for whatever plan they implemented tonight.

"You can take my car," Grayson said. "I'll ride shotgun with Gully in the van."

Grateful, she accepted his key fob. "Thanks." As she and Cole headed to the van, she battled a wave of frustration.

It was difficult to shake the sense of looming failure. The certainty that no matter which decision she made, it would backfire in her face.

And the worst thing of all was if that decision hurt someone she cared about. Any of her teammates, and of course Cole.

She wouldn't survive that dire consequence.

THEY RODE to Jina's police precinct with a strained silence hanging heavily between them. Cole felt as if he'd run a marathon, and the day had barely begun. Seeing first-hand the situations Jina and her team dealt with gave him a new appreciation for their role on the tactical team.

The recent bomb incident made his cold case look negligible. His job was to arrest bad guys, even if the crime had been committed twelve years ago. After all, there was no statute of limitations on murder.

But after today? Finding Brad's killer wasn't important. For all he knew, the killer was dead. Or in jail.

Keeping Jina safe was all that mattered.

"What are you thinking?" He broke the silence as they entered the Milwaukee city limits.

She shot him a quick glance before exiting the interstate. "Honestly? I'm not sure what to think. Other than I desperately want to draw this guy out of hiding."

"That's true for all of us." He wasn't sure which option was better either. "Maybe your boss will have an idea."

"I hope so." She tucked a strand of her hair behind her ear as they waited for the streetlight to change. "For lack of anything better, I'm still leaning toward the rental property in Timberland Falls."

"I hear you. I guess the worst that can happen is that he doesn't show."

She let out a low groan. "That's exactly what I'm afraid of. This guy is growing more reckless with every attempt. He planted that bomb with complete disregard for the innocent lives that could have been lost in the explosion. We need him to find me. And soon."

"He has been deliberately reckless," he agreed. "And seems to be gloating about how easily he's gotten away with everything so far."

"Tell me about it." She scowled while navigating the streets of the city. "He's really starting to make me mad."

She gestured to the windshield. "That's our precinct up ahead."

"I see it." The single-story building was similar in size and structure to his smaller department in Peabody. The difference was that the officers here covered only part of the sprawling city of Milwaukee. There were seven different districts here.

There was only one police department in Peabody.

Five minutes later, she parked Grayson's SUV in a small lot behind the building. He followed her to the side door, waiting as she punched in a keycode to gain access.

He recognized the tactical team's captain as he strode toward them. Rhy nodded at him, then turned to Jina. "Fill me in."

She did so with a brief yet comprehensive detailing of how they'd found the bomb, then neutralized it.

Rhy glanced at him. "The scent of gasoline tipped you off?"

"Yes, sir." Rhy wasn't his boss, but he had a commanding presence just the same. "He'd already started a fire at Jina's duplex using turpentine, so I searched for a possible incendiary device."

"Good call." Rhy scowled. "I don't like how he's changing his MO. Gunfire, arson, now a bomb? Who is this guy?"

"That's what we'd all like to know," Jina said. "Ex-cop or military."

Rhy nodded thoughtfully. "I've secured a conference room for us to use. Unfortunately, the rest of the team is tied up. Joe has them out at the scene of a large drug bust because there are multiple armed perps suspected to be in the area. So it's just you, Grayson, Cassidy, Zeke, and Flynn."

"And me," Cole spoke up. "I'm sticking with Jina until we have this guy behind bars."

"And you," Rhy agreed, then turned to lead the way to the conference room.

It didn't take long for the others to join them. Cassidy brought bottles of water and passed them out among the group. Zeke and Flynn had both his and Jina's bags. He reached for his, anxious to access his computer.

Going back to the gym where this all started made sense. It was the first attack against Jina, albeit a rather pathetic one. But maybe the perp hadn't anticipated Cole showing up to help her.

In hindsight, it seemed clear the assailant had planned to confront Jina at her place. And maybe Cole's arrival had thrown a monkey wrench into that attempt too.

While they waited for Grayson to arrive, he went back to the list of gym members with law enforcement background that Mike had provided. While Jina hadn't recognized any of the names aside from the two Timberland Falls cops, Oliver and Evan, it could easily be that one of the club members knew her.

And resented her for . . . what?

"Tell me about the team." He eyed Rhy who was seated at one end of the table. "Do cops go through a vetting process to become members?"

Rhy nodded, clearly following his train of thought. "Not a tryout or anything, but I tend to be selective when adding members to the team."

"Except for Roscoe, we've all been cops here in Milwaukee, prior to being transferred here," Jina added.

"Yeah, Roscoe was highly recommended by his cousin Cameron who was also an MPD cop. Speaking for myself, I was a little surprised Rhy took him on," Zeke said. "Why do you ask?"

"I was curious if Jina had gotten the job over someone else," Cole said to clarify his thought process. "Some guys can't stand being beaten out by a woman."

"There was only one candidate I didn't hire," Rhy said. "But Jina was already a member of the team. If Jeff Klapper has anyone to be upset with, it's Roscoe."

"I see." He shrugged. "I was hoping for another lead to follow up on." Then he glanced down at the list of gym members on his screen and almost choked. "Wait a minute, are you sure about that? Because Jeff Klapper is on the list." He lifted his head to scan the faces seated at the table around him. "Klapper belongs to Mike's MMA gym."

"He does?" Jina appeared surprised. "That's strange. I don't remember ever seeing him there."

"You go late in the evening, though, right?" He flushed a little as she arched a brow at how closely he'd watched her prior to the night of the shooting. "Maybe Klapper is an early bird."

"If he hasn't seen me there, why try to shoot me?" She shook her head. "Not sure we can pin this on him."

"Hold on, Jina," Rhy said. "We need all possible suspects on the table."

"Okay, but I had nothing to do with his not landing a spot on the team. That was all Roscoe."

The conference room door opened, revealing Grayson and another guy who was tall and lean, with brown hair and thick glasses. Cole noticed the guy looked at Cassidy first, then turned to Jina.

"Come in. Gabe, do you have something for us?" Rhy asked.

"Yes." Gabe pushed his glasses up on his nose in a

nervous gesture. "I've been digging into that guy who assaulted Jina in college, Rory Glick. I just heard back from the Tulsa cop who agreed to go over to Glick's last-known address to speak with him. He just let me know that Rory's parents haven't seen him in a few days."

"You're saying he could be here in Milwaukee." Rhy drummed his fingers on the table. "That's interesting."

"They don't know where he is, but yes, it's possible," Gabe said. "I've requested a search warrant to look at his recent debit and credit card purchases."

"Do you have enough evidence for that?" Cole asked.

"I think so. The guy hasn't shown up for his warehouse job and has a clear reason to hate Jina." Gabe shrugged. "I think we'll get it."

"Good work, Gabe," Rhy said. "Stay focused on Glick, we're relying on your expertise to tease out key information from his credit and debit reports. We can start digging into Jeff Klapper. His middle name is Thomas, and I think he lives in West Angelo."

As Rhy spoke, Cole used his computer to access Jeff Thomas Klapper's DMV records. "He does live in a small house in West Angelo. But he doesn't drive a black Honda."

"Why don't we head to the gym to see if he's there?" Cassidy asked.

"I'd rather call Mike, the owner first. He knows his members better than anyone." He pulled out his phone to make the call.

"This is Mike," the owner answered on the second ring.

"Hey, Mike, it's Cole. Do you know a guy named Jeff Klapper?"

"Sure, I know him, why?"

"Is he there, now?" Cole asked.

"Not that I noticed, he tends to come only on his days

off work, but I can check." There was a brief pause. "Why are you asking? I thought you and Jina didn't think any of my members were responsible for the shooting?"

"To be honest, we're running out of leads. We just need to cover all bases." There was a long moment of silence, indicating Mike wasn't buying that story. "Honestly, Mike, this is a guy we'd like to cross off our suspect list. Nothing for you to worry about." He hoped.

Mike let out a heavy sigh. "Fine. Lemme put you on hold for a moment." There was nothing but silence for a full sixty seconds. "Cole? You're in luck. Jeff is here."

"He is?" He pinned Jina with a hopeful look. "Can you keep him there until we arrive?"

"I'll try. But Jeff isn't one for small talk. Get here soon." Mike quickly ended the call.

"Let's go." Jina was already on her feet. "I'm sure a brief chat about where he's been over the past twenty-four hours will clear him."

"I'm coming with you," Grayson said. She didn't argue but tossed him the keys.

"Do you want more backup?" Zeke asked.

"I think three cops can handle it," Rhy said. "But before you go, Cole, send us that list of gym members. We'll keep looking at things from our end."

As Rhy rattled off his email address, Cole typed it in and hit send. Then shut the computer, leaving it on the table. He doubted the conversation with Klapper would take long, and they'd be back here within the hour.

As they drove to the MMA gym, he thought about the possibility of Rory Glick coming to Milwaukee to confront Jina. While he had the biggest reason to resent Jina, it seemed unlikely that he'd be smart enough to set a bomb, a fire, track her phone, and shoot at her.

If not Glick, then who? Klapper? Or someone else?

"Take the next exit," Jina told Grayson. The guy had pushed the speed limit so they wouldn't miss him. "Then head south."

"I've heard of the gym but never been inside," Grayson said.

"I like it." Jina frowned, then added, "At least I used to. Not sure after all of this."

When Grayson pulled into the parking lot, there were only a handful of vehicles scattered around. The hour was closing in on eleven in the morning, which wasn't peak gym hours for those who worked.

Grayson had barely stopped the car when Jina jumped out, eager to get inside. She moved to give him room when a crack of gunfire had them all dropping to the ground.

Another attempt in broad daylight! He glanced at Jina and could tell she was about to sprint toward the woods. Until more gunfire peppered the ground in front of them.

Pinning them in place with nowhere to hide.

CHAPTER FOURTEEN

What was with this guy? Jina was so over ducking from this perp's gunfire. She pulled her weapon, wishing once again that she had her sniper's rifle. Her scope would enable her to pinpoint this joker's location.

Wishing for the situation to be different was useless. They had to outsmart this guy.

How, she wasn't sure.

"Klapper?" Cole asked in a whisper.

"Must be. Mike may have tipped him off by mistake."

As suddenly as it had started, the barrage of gunfire stopped. There was nothing but a prolonged silence for several long moments. She glanced at Cole crouched beside her, both using the open rear passenger door as cover, then tipped her head toward the woods. "You go left, I go right."

"Not yet." He grabbed her arm with his free hand. He'd pulled his weapon too and was also prepared to return fire. "Could be a trap."

"This whole thing is a trap," she hissed in a low voice. "We need to get him!"

"Jina? Cole? Anyone hurt?" Grayson asked from the driver's side of the vehicle.

"Negative, we're good," she responded. Having a radio for communications would have been nice too. If the shooter was lingering nearby, he might be able to overhear their exchange. "You?"

"Fine here," Grayson confirmed. "I think our perp is in the woods behind the building."

"I'm sure he is," Cole agreed. "They're not deep but extend the length of the gym. A buffer of sorts between the back of the gym and the strip mall behind it."

"Understood," Grayson said. "What's the plan?"

"We need you to provide cover," Jina spoke up. "Cole and I will split up and try to find him."

There was a long moment as Grayson considered her request. Finally, he said, "Okay. Give me a minute to get into a better position."

Another long moment of silence hung between them. Jina battled a wave of frustration at the thought of this guy getting away yet again.

And now she felt certain their perp was Jeff Klapper. A fellow officer, a guy she barely knew wanted to kill her. It didn't make any sense, especially after all this time, but her only goal now was to grab him.

"I'm ready," Grayson said. "I'll take three shots, then you can go."

"Roger that." She tensed, waiting for the gunfire. Grayson was close enough that the sound was deafening, but the moment he'd fired the third and final shot, she sprinted away from the SUV to the right, trusting Cole to do his part.

She ran quickly but not silently. Klapper must have known they'd come after him and was probably already trying to make his getaway in the black Honda. The urge to derail his escape was strong, but once she reached the sparse wooded area, she paused to regroup.

Using a tree for cover, she swept her gaze over the area. There were about five cars parked in front of the strip mall, but a quick glance proved none were a black Honda without plates. A minivan, a sedan, and a black Ford SUV with plates, which gave her pause.

Had the shooter changed vehicles? Or had he parked his SUV behind the strip mall the way he'd done that first night?

Was that just thirty-six hours ago? It seemed like a lifetime.

She couldn't see Cole, so she made her way through the trees toward the front of the strip mall. Glancing down the tree line, she caught a glimpse of Cole about forty feet to her left.

The silence was nerve-racking. Had Mike called the police? Reports of gunfire, especially in the suburbs, usually garnered a quick response.

Catching Cole's gaze, she gestured to her right, wordlessly telling him she was going around to the back side of the strip mall. He nodded and gestured to the opposite side. Much like the first night they'd gone after this guy, they would circle the building and meet in the middle.

Sweeping one last gaze over the area, she ran toward the right end of the strip mall. Pausing at the corner, she edged along the building, looking for anything unusual.

But she didn't see anyone or a black SUV.

Upon reaching the opposite corner, she peered around it to scan the back. She'd expected to see the black Honda again, but there was nothing.

Not a car or a person. Absolutely nobody was back

there. Except for Cole, mirroring her movements on the other side of the building.

Where had the perp gone? He couldn't have disappeared into thin air.

She spun on her heel and ran quickly back to the front of the strip mall. The black Ford was still there, so she quickly approached, her weapon up and ready.

A door opened, and she swung around to face the person coming out. A woman screamed and threw up her hands, dropping her bag on the ground. "Don't shoot! Don't shoot!" she cried in alarm.

"I won't. I'm police officer Jina Wheeler." She lowered her weapon. "Did you see a man with a gun go past here?"

"What? No! A shooter?" The woman glanced around nervously.

"We've cleared the area, ma'am," Jina assured her. "Which vehicle is yours?"

"Th-the SUV?" The woman still looked terrified. Glancing at the ground, Jina noticed cosmetics had spilled from her bag.

"Sorry to frighten you," Jina said apologetically. "You're free to go."

The woman took a few steps to the car, then remembered her cosmetics. Jina suspected she had well over a hundred dollars' worth of products there and quickly bent to help her retrieve them.

Cole came over to join her. "Any sign of him?"

"No." She couldn't help sounding disgusted. "I don't get this Klapper dude. Why take shots at us in broad daylight?"

"A crime of opportunity." Cole shrugged. "He knows we're onto him. He waited here to pounce the minute we arrived."

"Yeah." She glanced around the strip mall area, then

sighed. "Let's go talk to Mike. Maybe he can shed some light on the sequence of events."

"Agree." Cole gestured for her to go ahead of him. "Keep your eyes peeled, though, in case we somehow missed him."

Taking the lead, she cut through the narrow swath of woods, heading over to where Grayson was still stationed near his now bullet-ridden SUV. She felt a twinge of regret over the hit Rhy's budget would take over this.

Again.

"He escaped?" Grayson asked.

"Seems that way." She holstered her weapon as the screech of police sirens filled the air. "Oh boy. The Brookland cops won't be happy to see us."

"I've updated Rhy on the situation," Grayson said. "He's heading here with Cassidy and Zeke. Flynn is still drilling down into Jeff Klapper's social media."

"I'm surprised he's on there, proves he's not very smart." She glanced at Cole. "Let's go see Mike."

"No need, he's watching from the doorway." Cole gestured to Mike, letting him know it was safe to come out. Mike left the sanctuary of the gym and hurried toward them.

"When did Klapper leave?" Jina demanded.

Mike looked surprised by her comment. "I asked him to stick around after he showered. Last I knew, he was still in the men's locker room when the gunfire rang out."

She turned back to the gym, eyeing the building thoughtfully. "Could he have left via the back without you seeing him?"

"Maybe. I can go back and check," Mike offered. "When I heard the gunfire, I told all the patrons working out to seek cover in the locker rooms until I told them the coast was clear."

"How many people total, aside from Klapper?" Jina asked.

"Only six or so," Mike said. "This isn't my peak time of the day."

Three Brookland police cruisers with red and blue lights flashing were headed their way. Jina knew they'd get stuck giving statements if they didn't get inside the gym. "Grayson, can you handle this while we find Klapper?"

"Go," Grayson said with a nod.

She grabbed Mike's arm and gestured to the main entrance. "We need to hurry."

Mike didn't hesitate to move toward the gym. She and Cole flanked him on either side. The MMA gym was nothing fancy, which was exactly what she liked the most about it.

"This way," Mike said, heading straight toward the men's locker room. He glanced at her, and added, "No women in here today."

"Understood." She knew she was one of the few female members. She let Mike go in first, but then crowded in behind him, not caring if some of the guys were half dressed or not. She didn't care about that.

She needed to find Jeff Klapper.

"Where is he?" she asked as Mike frowned, glancing around in confusion. She didn't trust her memory to recognize him.

"I guess he's not here." Mike lifted his hands in a help-less gesture. "I know he came this way, though." The gym owner gave her a chagrined look. "I'm sorry I let you down."

She managed a smile, even though she wanted to pound her fists on the lockers. "Not your fault." She nodded at the six guys standing around looking concerned. "Sorry to interrupt. Obviously, there has been some gunfire outside, but the local police have arrived, and the shooter has left the area. You can head out if you'd like."

"Man, this place is really going downhill," a handsome arrogant guy muttered harshly as he brushed past her.

"Not true. None of this is Mike's fault," she said sharply. "It's mine."

Mr. Arrogant glanced back at her as if he wanted to say something more, then must have thought better of it. Without another word, he disappeared through the doorway. Her comment seemed to shut the rest of them up as they filed suit.

It burned to know Mike's business would take a hit after this. Granted, two episodes of gunfire in two days was a lot. Even though many of the gym members were cops, they wouldn't want to hang out at a place where random shootings were rampant.

Maybe she could convince the rest of the team to join the gym to make up for any memberships Mike might lose after this.

She followed Cole and Mike out of the locker room, then paused to glance over at the women's locker room. After being inside the men's, she could attest to how much smaller it was in comparison. Which was logical as there weren't nearly as many female members from what she could tell.

In most of her recent visits, she'd had the locker room to herself. A far cry from other gyms she'd used to belong to.

Turning, she pushed the locker room door open and shouldn't have been disappointed it appeared empty. Still, she went all the way inside to check the shower area too.

And found nothing.

Where in the world had Jeff Klapper gone?

Emerging from the locker room, she saw Mike and Cole talking in low voices near the front door. She turned to head back toward Mike's small office area, determined to check the rear door.

Buildings were required by fire codes to have more than one exit. Maybe being a member of Rhy's tactical team had made her overly paranoid, and the first time she'd toured the gym prior to paying for an annual membership, she'd asked Mike to show her the rear exit. Thankfully, he'd obliged.

As she passed Mike's office, she heard her name. Glancing to the right where the storeroom was located, she saw Duncan lurking there. His eyes were wide, his scarred face mostly covered by his beard. She remembered Mike telling her Duncan had been in a work-related accident that had caused him to require surgery for deep facial lacerations. She hadn't noticed them much before, but the white lines looked more pronounced up close.

"Jina, this way." Duncan gestured for her to come closer. "I saw a guy leaving out the back before the shooting started."

"You did?" She quickly hurried over to join him. "Do you know Jeff Klapper? I think he's the guy who's been targeting me."

"Yeah, I know Jeff," Duncan said with a nod. "He was here earlier, talking to Mike. I wasn't included in their conversation, but I could tell Mike was concerned. Come with me, I'll show you where he went."

No surprise Klapper had gone out the back, just as she'd suspected. She nodded, and asked, "Does he drive a black Honda SUV?"

"Yep. I've seen it a couple of times," Duncan admitted.

"I was surprised when Mike said he needed to talk to Klapper. I had a feeling it was because you considered him a suspect."

"You guessed right. Mike was trying to hold him here so I could confront him." She wished they could have gotten there a few minutes earlier.

"If I had known that, I would have grabbed him," Duncan said with a frown.

"Not your fault." She might have included him but hadn't expected Duncan to be there. In her experience, he mostly worked late evening and night shifts. And those were the shifts she usually came in to work out too.

She followed Duncan farther down the hall toward the exit. There was no window on the door like there was in the front, so she couldn't see outside. As they reached the doorway, Duncan abruptly turned and jammed his hand into her side.

A hand that held a gun.

"What are you doing?" She tried to reach for her weapon, but Duncan had already removed it from her holster, an evil grin playing across his features.

"We're taking a little ride," he said in a harsh whisper. "Just you and me, Jina."

Realization dawned a fraction of a second too late. Klapper wasn't the shooter. Duncan was.

And she'd foolishly walked right into his trap.

"WHERE WAS Klapper when the gunfire went off?" Cole asked, trying to follow Mike's timeline.

"I asked him to stay and talk to me, but he claimed he

had to go. That he needed to take a shower and then hit the road because he was running late," Mike explained. "I was about to follow him into the men's locker room when I heard the gunfire. That's when I went out into the main gym to tell the others to get into the locker room too."

Cole frowned. "How much time passed between Klapper going into the locker room and the sound of gunfire?"

"Barely a minute, maybe less."

That wasn't nearly enough time for Klapper to have been their shooter.

"I'm sorry if I messed up," Mike said. "I tried to get him to stick around."

"He's probably not our guy anyway, so don't worry about it," Cole assured him. He ran his frustrated hand through his hair. "Unfortunately, that only means we still have no idea who this guy is or why he wants to hurt Jina."

"I wish you were closer to finding this guy. I'm going to lose business over this." Mike looked depressed.

"Hey, we'll find him." He clapped Mike on the shoulder as Rhy, Cassidy, and Zeke approached the gym. "And once we do, there won't be a reason for people to avoid coming here."

"I'm not sure about that."

He didn't ask if Mike wasn't sure they'd catch the guy or if the gym members would return once the danger was over.

And decided now wasn't the time to ask.

"Did you find Jeff Klapper?" Rhy demanded.

"No, and based on Mike's timeline, he's not our guy." He quickly filled the captain in on the sequence of events.

"Where's Jina?" Zeke asked.

Cole turned to glance behind him, surprised she wasn't there.

"I think she ducked into the female locker room," Mike said.

"I'll check on her." Cassidy brushed past him.

"If Klapper isn't our guy, then how in the world did he know you, Jina, and Grayson were on your way here?" Rhy asked with a scowl. "Something isn't adding up."

"I know, that's bothering me too." He didn't want to put Mike in the hot seat but turned to face the gym owner. "Was there anything else unusual prior to hearing the gunfire?"

"No. I was reconciling my monthly statement for last month when you called," Mike said. "I dropped everything to head out to find Klapper."

Cole masked his disappointment. It wasn't Mike's fault. He turned back to Rhy and Zeke. "Jina and I split up as Grayson provided cover. We went through the woods all the way back around the strip mall. There was nothing back there. Unfortunately, it seems as if our perp escaped before we could get a visual."

"I hear you." Rhy grimaced and glanced behind him. "The local police are here and need your statements. When we're finished, we can head back to the precinct to plan our next move."

"Do you think setting Jina up at the Timberland Falls property is still a go?" Zeke asked.

"Unless we can come up with something better, yeah," Rhy said. "I'm open to other options."

"Jina's not in the locker room." Cassidy's expression held concern as she joined them.

"Maybe she went into my office?" Mike turned to head that way.

"No, we'll go." Cole grabbed his arm to stop him. "We're armed."

"Yeah, sure." Mike moved out of the way. "My office is on the left, and the storeroom is to the right."

Cole took the lead, as he was closest, but Zeke, Cassidy, and Rhy were not far behind. Holding his weapon ready, he crossed the room toward Mike's office. Finding the door hanging ajar, he hung back as he kicked it open.

Empty.

Without hesitation, he moved farther down the hall. The storeroom door was also hanging open, and when he kicked that door open, he found it empty too.

The knot in his stomach tightened as he continued down the hall to the rear exit. Maybe he was overreacting. Jina could have come this way solely to check the area for herself.

But that didn't stop him from praying she was okay. He pushed the door open, then hung back to sweep the area with his gaze.

And found nothing.

Battling another wave of fear, he ran outside, looking from left to right.

"Maybe she's out front, already giving her statement," Rhy said, coming up beside him.

He nodded, turning to head around the corner to the front of the gym. There were lots of people milling about now. A few of the gym members they'd released from the locker room were still standing around, along with what seemed like even more cops than had initially shown up to the scene.

"I don't see her," Zeke said with concern.

"I don't either," Cassidy said. "Her blond hair usually stands out."

Cole continued forward, taking his time to look methodically from one person to the next until he, too, understood Jina wasn't out there.

Then he turned to glance back at the wooded area. Had something out there drawn her attention?

"We need to check the strip mall again." Without waiting for a response, he broke into a run. Apprehension clawed at him, telling him something wasn't right.

The same way it had when he'd been interviewing Henry and Erma Crow.

He burst through the trees, searching desperately for Jina's blond hair or the black Honda. When he didn't see them, he continued moving to the back of the strip mall, still praying for God to keep Jina safe.

He stopped abruptly when he noticed the area behind the strip mall was deserted.

Where could she be?

"Cole?" He turned to meet Rhy's grim expression. "We need to head back to the gym. That's the last place she was seen."

The last place Jina was seen alive. A warning chill slid down his spine, and he glanced at his watch. She'd only been missing for a few minutes, but that was more than enough time for the perp to grab her, kill her, and dump the body.

Please, Lord, protect her! Please keep her safe in Your loving arms!

"Cole?" Rhy searched his gaze, as if sensing how close he was to losing it.

He managed to nod and quickly joined the rest of Jina's teammates as they jogged back to the gym.

"Detective Cole Roberts?" He recognized Brookland police officer Howard scowling at him. "I need to talk to you."

"Not now." He went around Howard and his cohort Tyson to head back inside the gym. Jina had been there, but now she was gone.

What were they missing?

He found Mike sitting at his desk. "I need to know the names of everyone who'd been inside when the shooting started."

"I already told you that," Mike said, looking defeated. "It was a slow day. Those guys in the locker room were the only ones here. Oh, and Jeff Klapper too."

"And you're sure there wasn't anyone else?" It was all he could do not to scream at the gym owner. "If you were in your office, how would you know who was out there and who wasn't?"

"I checked them in, then when there was a lull in the action, I came back here." Mike gestured to the computer. "I mentioned before that I have a camera that shows me when someone comes inside."

"Roll the video," Cole said. "And hurry."

"Sure." Mike tapped a few keys, bringing the video up on the screen. He went back to the time before the shooting, then hit the play button.

Cole watched as one guy, then another came into the gym. Then he saw Duncan. "Stop the video. You didn't mention Duncan."

"Oh yeah. Well, he works here and gets the perk of a free gym membership." Mike frowned. "He's not usually here so early, though."

Alarm bells went off in the back of Cole's mind. "Fast-forward the video, see if he leaves the gym through the front door."

Mike did so, then sat back in his chair with a dazed

expression on his face. "Duncan didn't leave out the front. And he wasn't in the locker room either."

Cole was already turning away. Duncan was their shooter, and he had Jina.

There wasn't much time left to find them.

CHAPTER FIFTEEN

"Why are you doing this, Duncan?" Jina shot him a quick glance, then turned her attention to the road before them. He'd forced her behind the wheel at gunpoint, then tossed her weapon outside the car once they'd left the strip mall.

They were in a white Dodge minivan that had been parked right in plain sight in front of the strip mall. It wasn't the black Honda she and Cole had tried to find. Considering how Duncan had swapped vehicles, she feared Cole, Rhy, and the rest of her team would never find her.

"You don't recognize me at all, do you?" Duncan's tone was conversational, but his intent was not. He held the weapon aimed at her side where he could easily shoot her if necessary.

Recognize him? "No, I'm sorry, I don't." She risked another glance. "I assume we met somewhere besides the gym."

"You could say that. Turn right. Head to the freeway."

Heading to the freeway was the last thing she wanted to do, it would only put more miles between her and the rest of her team. How long would it take for them to figure out Duncan had taken her a gunpoint?

Too long. There was no point in waiting for them. She'd need to rescue herself.

"Duncan, I'm sorry I don't remember you. Why not tell me where we met?" She gripped the steering wheel tightly. "You're going to kill me anyway, so what's the harm?"

"Think, Jina." His voice was a low hiss. "I did everything for you, supported you in every way possible, and you left me without a second thought."

Left him? Then the memory clicked. Her friend Jaxon Palmer. The guy who'd tried to convince her to move to Nashville with him. Risking a quick glance at him, she noted the resemblance. The scars and beard had changed his appearance to a certain degree.

"Jaxon, I'm sorry." She worked to keep her tone even, despite the anger building within. He had done all of this because she'd considered him a friend, but not someone she loved enough to move across the country for? What was wrong with him? Besides the obvious. "I didn't want to leave my sister, Shelly. Certainly, you can understand that."

"You've always been selfish, thinking only about yourself." He sounded disgusted with her. "You have no idea the things I did for you."

"I don't understand. We were friends. We hung out together." She had no idea what he meant but figured it was best to keep him talking. She didn't know where he'd planned to take her but understood she needed to make her move prior to getting there. Too bad they were driving the minivan rather than her Jeep.

Wrecking it was her only option. Even that was risky, Duncan—or rather Jaxon—could squeeze the trigger, killing her as she stomped on the brake and wrenched the wheel.

Regardless, she wouldn't do that until he told her to get off the interstate. She found herself praying she wouldn't take any innocent lives with her in her attempt to escape.

"I killed him for you!" Jaxon shouted the words. "Don't you understand? I did everything possible to protect you, and you turned your back on me. We were supposed to be together, Jina."

"Who did you kill?" Then she knew. Brad Crow, her stalker. She'd told Jaxon all about the guy staring at her.

"Why would you do that?" She turned to gape at him. "I didn't ask you to kill anyone!"

"You're so clueless," he said with annoyance. "I was headed to your place the night that creepy Brad Crow tried to get into your window. I practically ran into him as he darted out into the road. He began babbling about how you'd shot him when he tried climbing into your bedroom. So I finished the job. Hit him in the head with a baseball bat, then buried his body. For you, Jina. To protect you!" He was screaming at her again, as if he were on the verge of losing his mind.

And maybe he was. No sane person would kill someone expecting to be thanked for it. She had no idea Jaxon had killed Brad. Or that he'd been coming out to see her. The incident was a long time ago. What had Jaxon been doing all this time? What had brought him back to Wisconsin?

Unless he hadn't left at all? The thought gave her a chill.

She must be the only woman in the planet who'd had two stalkers in one lifetime.

"I'm so sorry. I didn't mean to upset you. You're a good friend, Jax." She tried her best to smile reassuringly, as if she wasn't horrified by every word that came out of his mouth. "Please, put the gun away so we can talk this through."

"You had your chance," he said in a dismissive tone. "We talked about Nashville, getting jobs and enjoying the music scene. But that didn't last long, did it?"

"I'm sorry," she repeated.

"You said that eleven years ago too. Remember? The week after graduation when you told me you were moving to Madison to attend college?" His voice changed to a falsetto. "I'm sorry, Jaxon, but things have changed. I can't come with you."

She remembered. The same words he'd thrown back at her outside the American Lodge. There had to be more to this than her refusal to relocate to Nashville. But just then, he said, "Take the exit before that farmer's field you drove into."

"Sure, Jax. Whatever you say." She glanced at him again, disconcerted to find him staring at her intently. As if she were an insect he was about to dissect.

"Aren't you going to ask what happened?" His mind was like a Ping-Pong ball, jumping from one subject to the next. "About my scars?"

"Mike mentioned you were in a work-related accident." She wished she'd paid more attention to Duncan, er, Jaxon, before now.

"I was hit by a car. I became a cop just like you, but it didn't work out as well as I thought. Did you know I was also there the night you laughed and flirted with that guy at the party? Oh look, there's our exit up ahead."

It took every ounce of willpower she had not to react to the news that he was at the party in Madison where she'd been with Rory. Jaxon was a cop? He'd been following her for years? Did he know how her night with Rory had ended? His admitting to killing Brad combined with this latest tidbit of information was too much for her brain to comprehend.

Ignoring him, she focused on the exit, eyeing the vehicles around them. When it was clear none of them were going to get off the interstate, she momentarily took her foot off the gas, turning the wheel toward the ramp.

One. Two. Three. She abruptly hit the brake and cranked the wheel to the left, causing the minivan tires to squeal in protest. The car spun one hundred and eighty degrees. She hit the gas again, still cranking on the wheel. Jaxon screamed obscenities, but then the car was tumbling over, turning upside down like her Jeep had, while sliding into the deep gully below.

The airbags deployed, smashing her in the face with enough force to bring tears to her eyes. Twice in a matter of days was a lot. In the back of her mind, she prayed the airbag deploying on his side had caused him to lose the gun. The seat belt cut painfully across her chest, and her head throbbed with the beat of her heart. She willed herself to stay conscious.

The good news? No sound of gunfire. At least, not yet.

Dazed, she clawed at the seatbelt, desperate to get away. She released the restraint and crawled out of the broken window when she felt Jaxon's hand grab her ankle.

No! Viciously kicking with her other foot, she used her elbows to dig into the ground to jerk away. Her foot finally hit its mark, and the hand around her ankle fell away.

Did he still have the gun? She was afraid she was about to find out.

Pulling herself away from the wreck, she staggered to her feet. Without looking behind her, she ran up the exit ramp to the interstate. It was slow going, every muscle in her body screamed in pain, and the incline wasn't helping.

"Jina!" Hearing Jaxon shout her name, she hunched her shoulders and ducked her head in a vain effort to make herself a smaller target.

An SUV started down the exit ramp, coming straight for her. She raised her arms to flag it down, gaping in shock when she saw Cole behind the wheel.

Before she could thank God for sending him to help her, another gunshot rang out.

———

"JINA!" Cole stomped on the brake, even as a crack of gunfire echoed around them. The bullet missed the car, but it was a warning that Duncan was still armed and dangerous. Thankfully, Jina was on the passenger side of the vehicle. She wrenched the door open and jumped in. "Go!"

Knowing Rhy was mere seconds behind him, he didn't hesitate to hit the gas, speeding as fast as he dared past the upside-down minivan. When they'd safely cleared it, he turned toward her. "Are you hurt?"

"No." It was clearly a lie as she had cuts on her arms and a whopper of a bruise darkening the skin around her left eye. "Duncan is really Jaxon, an old friend of mine."

"He is?" When they were fifty yards past the minivan, he pulled over to the side of the road, threw the car into park, and reached for his phone. "Rhy? I have Jina, and she's okay. Perp is armed and seeking refuge within the damaged minivan."

"I see it. Thanks for the intel." Rhy's voice was remarkably calm. Cole had to give the guy credit for keeping a cool head in the face of an emergency. "Zeke and Cassidy are here too. We've got this. Sit tight with Jina."

"Roger that." He ended the call, filled with relief that the nightmare was almost over.

"No, we can't sit here. I want to help." Jina pushed at her door, as if forgetting that it was still locked. "We need to back them up."

"Hold on, where's your weapon?" He lightly grabbed her wrist, but she recoiled so badly he abruptly let her go. Whatever had transpired in the car with Duncan had messed with her mind. "Take a breath and think. What can you do?"

She lowered her chin to her chest, taking several deep, ragged breaths. Then nodded. "You're right. I need a gun." She looked him dead in the eye. "Give me yours."

Okay, that was not what he'd wanted to hear. "You've been in a crash. You're not thinking clearly. Let Rhy and your teammates handle this."

"Are you going to loan me your gun or not?" she demanded.

There was no point in arguing. He unholstered his weapon and handed it to her butt first. "Fine, I'm coming with you."

She gave a jerky nod and unlocked the door. She slid out of the car, moving more slowly than usual, which gave him time to go around the front to join her.

"Lean on me." He wrapped an arm around her waist.

"I'm fine. We can't let him get away." As if imagining that fate, she appeared stronger and more determined. They quickly crossed the grassy area to look down into the gully. "He's going to make a run for it."

She'd no sooner spoken the words when a dark figure popped up from behind the wreck and turned toward them. Even from here, Cole could see the gun in Duncan's hand.

"Don't move!" Jina shouted. "Drop it!"

Duncan didn't listen. He lifted the weapon toward Jina. She fired two shots in rapid succession, striking Duncan center mass.

He dropped like a rock. Cole arched a brow at Jina. "That's some good shooting considering you're using a strange gun."

She shrugged, then moved toward the fallen man. Rhy, Zeke, and Cassidy had been converging on the vehicle from all sides, but somehow, Jina got there first.

After kicking the gun farther away from Duncan's outstretched hand, she knelt to feel a pulse. "He's alive. Call 911 for an ambulance."

"They're en route," Rhy said. "Do we need to do CPR?"

"He still has a pulse, but it's weak." Jina balled up Duncan's shirt and pressed it against his abdominal wound.

"I'll take over," Cassidy said, nudging her aside. "You look like you've been through the wringer."

"Thanks." It was a testament to how bad Jina must have felt that she let Cassidy take over. She struggled to her feet, then turned to face Cole. "Like I said, Duncan is really Jaxon Palmer. He admitted to killing Brad Crow."

Stunned, he stared at her. "Why would he do that?"

She rubbed the temple beside her darkening eye. "Jaxon worked with me at the custard stand. I mentioned seeing the creepy guy staring at me. Apparently, Jaxon thought he was helping me by killing Brad after he fled my parents' farmhouse. I didn't get the entire story, but he was mad that I wouldn't relocate to Nashville with him. I thought he'd moved on, but apparently not. I don't know the details, but he claimed a car crash required him to have surgery on his face. It makes me wonder if he'd used that as an excuse to find me again."

He glanced down at Jaxon/Duncan. He believed Jina

was telling the truth, but her story was like something out of a movie. He found himself praying Jaxon/Duncan wouldn't die so that they could convince him to talk.

He needed something to corroborate her story.

"Yeah, I get it." Jina's voice was flat. "To be honest, it's hard for me to believe it too." With that, she turned and walked toward Rhy. "Hey, boss. We need to talk. There's a lot I need to fill you in on."

Rhy lifted a brow at Cole, who could only shrug. What could he say? His cold case and her current situation had intersected in a way he had never imagined.

Which meant he needed to proceed with caution until he could verify that Duncan was really Jaxon Palmer and that he'd killed Brad Crow.

Watching as Rhy and Jina walked away from the minivan, Cole had never felt so alone.

"I COULD USE SOME ASPIRIN," Jina said, eyeing Rhy across his desk at the precinct. Several hours had passed since she'd crashed the minivan and shot Jaxon Palmer. Once the Lifeline Air Rescue helicopter had carried Jaxon up through the sky toward Trinity Medical Center for emergency surgery, she'd accompanied Rhy to the precinct. She'd washed the dirt and blood from her skin, then changed into a spare set of clothing she always kept in her locker.

They'd been talking for an hour. In some ways, telling her boss everything was incredibly freeing. She hadn't realized how much her secret had weighed on her mind. And she was still upset with herself for not recognizing that Duncan was Jaxon. Looking back, though, the timing was such that she should have suspected him. Duncan had been working out at the gym the day she'd joined. Then he took the second-shift manager position. From then on, she'd seen him there every single time she'd gone to work out.

And he'd also watched as she was victorious over sparring with the guys who'd hit on her.

She could only imagine that he'd gotten sick of her coming out on top. In a way he never could. Unfortunately, they may never know the entire story.

Her main concern was the man seated across from her. Being a part of Rhy's team was the best thing that had ever happened to her, and she didn't want to lose them. Yet she refused to lie. Especially now that Duncan was really Jaxon, and he'd tried to kill her.

Rhy opened his desk drawer and removed a bottle of painkillers. He slid the bottle across the desk, and she gratefully downed three of them with a healthy slug of water. There was a long silence as Rhy thought about everything she'd said.

"The problem as I see it is that you need Jaxon to survive his surgery long enough to be interviewed by Roberts, where he will hopefully confess to murder."

"Yes, sir." She grimaced. "I doubt he'll cooperate. If Jaxon lawyers up, Cole has only my word to weigh against Jaxon's."

"True, but Jaxon kidnapped you at gunpoint and made several other attempts against you." Rhy grinned. "Turns out, he didn't clean up after himself as well as he thought. As soon as we had Duncan/Jaxon as a suspect, I sent Mitch over to investigate. Mitch found a rag damp with paint thinner in the basement of his home, and his fingerprints were found on the inside of the door handle in the abandoned black Honda SUV. Oh, and that vehicle was stolen three days ago. By the time we process his weapon for ballistics, I'm sure we'll have more evidence against him."

"That's good news." She felt lighter knowing Rhy was on her side. But her heart ached over the way Cole had looked so skeptical when she claimed Jaxon had killed Brad.

He hadn't believed her.

Once, she wouldn't have blamed him. But the hours they'd spent together should have been proof that she wouldn't blithely break the law. She wasn't the same person now as she had been when she was seventeen and scared to death upon seeing a man crawl through her bedroom window.

And too uncertain of herself to report the incident to the police. The way she should have.

Now she'd fallen in love with a man who believed her to be capable of cold-blooded murder. Of course, shooting Jaxon when he lifted his weapon toward them didn't help matters. An action she had taken in self-defense, but that didn't always mean anything. Cops were held to a higher standard.

She knew Cole looked at her differently now. Ironic that she had begun to feel God's reassuring presence just as the man who'd convinced her to believe in Him had walked away.

"I'd like to go home." As soon as she said the words, she realized she couldn't go back to the burned duplex. She winced, then added, "I'll check with Cass, see if I can stay in her guest room."

"You're welcome to bunk at the homestead," Rhy offered. "We have lots of room."

"No thank you." She appreciated his support but knew he had a wife and daughter, not to mention a baby on the way. She wouldn't be comfortable spending that much time with her boss. She pushed herself to her feet, trying not to wince. "Is there anything else?"

"That's enough for now. You're on administrative leave, though, until the incident with Jaxon has been investigated." He raked a critical gaze over her. "You look like you need a few days off."

"Thank you." She turned and left Rhy's office. She expected to see Cassidy, Flynn, or Zeke waiting for her, but there was no sign of them.

Her phone was in her overnight bag, which she'd left in Grayson's shot-up SUV. She could use one of the landlines, but needing fresh air, she headed outside.

Cole pushed away from the SUV he'd used to rescue her, and to her surprise, he had her overnight bag in hand. "Hey."

"Hey." Disconcerted by his presence, she stepped closer. "I was just looking for my phone to get a rideshare."

"I'll drive you." He handed her the overnight bag. "I figured you needed a place to stay."

And he was offering what? For her to stay with him? Fat chance.

"I'll be fine." She narrowed her gaze. "I wouldn't want to compromise your case."

He sighed, raking his fingers through his dark-brown hair. "You must know that cow has already escaped from the barn."

"Farm humor," she deadpanned. "That's hilarious."

"I love you." When she snapped her head up to stare at him, he moved close enough to capture her hand in his. "I went crazy after you were kidnapped. I know you didn't kill anyone, and I have prayed nonstop that Jaxon Palmer will survive long enough for me to prove it to my boss. And the DA's office. And anyone else who needs to know the truth."

"How can you be so sure?"

"Because you told Jaxon not to do it and then waited for him to raise his weapon before taking the shot." He shook his head ruefully. "Trust me, most cops would have fired sooner. I probably would have if you hadn't taken my weapon. It was so obvious he wouldn't stop until he'd killed you."

She was surprised but secretly glad. The knot of tension faded. "Say it again."

"I believe you. I know you didn't kill—"

"Not that. The first part." She placed her hand in the center of his chest, shocked to feel the strong thumping beat of his heart. "The most important part."

"I love you. I know it's too fast, and you've made it clear you don't like to date, but I love you." He searched her gaze. "From the very beginning, I risked my career for you, Jina. And I'll keep doing that because you're the only thing that matters."

"Who said I don't like dating?" She couldn't help but smile. "I love you too, Cole. And I've never said that to another man in my entire life."

"You humble me," he whispered, drawing her into his arms. "I never thought I'd feel this way again. I guess God had other plans for me."

"I'm very grateful God brought us together." She wrapped her arms around his neck and pulled his head down for a long kiss.

Losing herself in his embrace was far too easy. Scary that she'd never felt this way before, while Cole had married his first love.

"Don't do that," he whispered. "I can tell you're allowing self-doubt to creep in, but there's no need. I love you very much."

"You seem to know me pretty well considering we've only met what, two days ago?" She pulled back to look up into his dark-brown eyes.

"Two days can be a lifetime when dodging bullets," he said with a smile. "Besides, it's not as if I didn't notice you at the gym. I also asked Mike about you."

She shook her head, smiling back. "I noticed you too. But I didn't ask Mike about you. In fact, I was convinced you were married, so I purposefully stayed away."

"I was married, but that was a long time ago." His expression sobered. "You've had a lot of bad experiences with men, Jina. I don't want to rush you into anything. We'll take things slow and easy."

"I'd like that." She was touched by his willingness to meet her more than halfway. "Maybe I could ask you out on a date. Like dinner tonight? I'm starved."

He threw his head back and laughed.

"What's so funny?" She frowned. "I thought you wanted to go out on a date!"

"I do, and I'd be honored to accept your offer of a date. Dinner sounds perfect. Anyplace you'd like to go works for me." He continued to chuckle, then kissed her again. "I love you so much."

"I love you too." She still wasn't sure why he'd found her comment so funny, but before she could say anything, a car pulled up next to them.

"Jina, it's time to stop kissing Cole," Cassidy said from the passenger seat. Zeke snickered at the comment. "Rhy mentioned you need a place to stay. My guest room is yours for as long as you need it."

"Oh, ah, thanks." She flushed and glanced at Cole who nodded. "I'll be in touch. We, um, have dinner plans."

Instead of looking disappointed, Cassidy did a quick fist pump. "Yes! I knew it. I knew you'd fall for the right guy."

"That makes one of us," she muttered. If anyone had told her she'd be going on a real dinner date with Cole Roberts, she'd have laughed in their face.

"Give me your address and I'll bring her by later, okay?" Cole said.

Cassidy rattled it off. Zeke waved, then pulled away.

Leaving her and Cole alone once again.

"Where would you like to go?" Cole opened the car door for her. She tossed her overnight bag in, realizing she had no idea. Her idea of meals was eating at Rosie's Diner or fast food.

"Um." She racked her brain for a nice restaurant.

Cole chuckled, then brushed a kiss on her mouth. "I know the perfect place. You like Italian, right?"

"Love it."

"There's a great Italian restaurant called Mario's a few miles from here. It's a weeknight, so they shouldn't be too busy."

"Sounds great." She slid into the passenger seat. "Thanks, Cole."

"My pleasure." He started the engine. "Slow and easy. No pressure."

She nodded, but deep down, she knew there was no reason for him to treat her like some porcelain doll that might break.

She was tough and resilient. As was Cole. She was pretty sure she'd be able to handle a relationship with him, despite her lack of experience with this sort of thing. She trusted Cole to catch her if she fell, and vice versa.

Together, they made a great team.

EPILOGUE

Three weeks later . . .

Cole finished his final report on Bradley Crow's murder and sent it to Lieutenant Bell. By God's grace, Jaxon Palmer had survived the surgery to remove the two bullets Jina had fired into his abdomen. The guy was looking at a long recovery, but Cole had gotten everything he'd wanted.

It had taken time to find Jaxon's mother, who had an unfortunate drinking problem, to get the information he'd needed to nail the lid on the guy's coffin. Jaxon's mother recognized the remnant of the wool blanket that had been used to wrap Brad's body as one belonging to her son. She'd also admitted he pretty much did whatever he wanted without any supervision from her.

Surprisingly, he'd learned Jaxon had become a cop, the same way Jina had. Maybe he had viewed that as the best way to win her back. Unfortunately, he'd been run over by a car as two perps had tried to escape a drug bust, his face and several bones in his body sustaining significant damage. The incident had ended Jaxon's short career. His rehab had been long and laborious, and from what Cole could tell, the guy had spent his time convalescing by obsessing over Jina.

After being released from all medical care, he'd changed his name to become Duncan Granger. Again, Cole surmised that the guy had thought starting over with a new identity would enable him to get close to Jina. Jaxon now Duncan had taken the second-shift manager role so that he could be there during the times of day she went there the most. But it soon became obvious that Jina wasn't interested. And the way she bested the guys at sparring had made Jaxon seethe with anger.

Jaxon had once again stalked Jina, this time to get her out of the picture, permanently. His major flaw was that he wanted her to know he was the one who'd done all of this. He wanted credit for the brilliance of his attacks. Instead of just killing her outright, he'd taken her away from the gym at gunpoint. Which had led to his downfall.

But the greatest find was the baseball bat that Jaxon had kept over all these years. He'd been so arrogant in his plan to avoid being caught that he'd kept the weapon and hadn't bothered to clean it. The lab had just finalized the DNA report matching the trace of blood and skin cells on the blunt end of the bat to that of Brad Crow.

Faced with all the evidence against him, Jaxon had accepted a plea deal. He'd taken the second-degree murder charge with a sentence of twenty years behind bars.

Case closed. At least on his part. He couldn't help but smile in knowing that Rhy was building a second case against the guy. Kidnapping, attempted murder, and arson. Even one of those charges would ensure Jaxon/Duncan would spend the rest of his life in prison.

Pushing away from his desk, he reached for his phone to

call Jina. "I'm heading over to pick you up," he said, turning to leave the Peabody precinct.

"I'm ready." She sounded cheerful.

"Great. See you soon." They'd taken to having dinner twice a week at Mario's restaurant. He patted his pocket, making sure the ring was there. It might be too soon for her, and if so, that was okay. He figured he'd ask her every couple of weeks, hoping she'd feel confident enough in his love for her to say yes.

Eventually.

Jina was waiting outside Cassidy's condo when he pulled up. She was dressed in a long, flowing, orange-patterned skirt topped with a solid orange sweater.

"Wow." He had never seen her dressed up like this. Jina was drop-dead gorgeous wearing a stained sweatshirt and holey sweatpants. He'd learned she tended to downplay her looks, maybe a holdover from the unwanted attention she'd gotten first from Brad Crow, then Rory, and finally Jaxon. This? The flowery skirt was a complete shift from the norm. "You look incredible."

"Thanks." She blushed as she smoothed her hand over the skirt. "Cassidy took me shopping. I had to ditch all my old clothes because they reeked of smoke, so I decided to start over."

"I love you no matter what you wear." He kissed her for a long moment, then forced himself to release her. "Let's go."

"Just a minute." She grasped his hand. "I have something I need to ask you."

"Okay, but you should know the case is over." He wasn't sure where she was going with this and hoped to reassure her. "There's no need to worry. You're in the clear."

"Not that." She looked up at him. "I love you, and well,

I'm hoping that maybe, um, someday, we might, you know . . ." She shrugged, then said, "Make it official."

His heart melted. He pulled out the ring and dropped to one knee. "Jina, will you please marry me?"

"You bought a ring?" She looked shocked. "When?"

"The day after our first date." He slowly rose to his feet. "Is that a yes?"

"Yes. Yes!" She threw herself into his arms. "I love you so much."

"I love you too." He kissed her again, then had to grin when he realized Cassidy was watching them through the window. He stepped back and slid the diamond ring on her finger. "Time to have dinner, soon-to-be Mrs. Jina Roberts."

"I'm more than ready to eat, soon-to-be Mr. Cole Wheeler," she countered with a smirk. "After all, I asked you first."

He couldn't help but laugh as he held her close. He didn't care if she took his name or not.

Nothing mattered as long as he could share the rest of his life with her.

I HOPE you've enjoyed Jina and Cole's story! I've had so much fun writing this Oath of Honor series. Are you ready to read *Zeke?* Click here!

DEAR READER

Thanks so much for reading my Oath of Honor series. I'm truly blessed to have wonderful readers like you. I hope you enjoyed Jina and Cole's story. I've been having so much fun bringing the Finnegans and even the Callahans back into these books. *Zeke* will be available soon, followed by *Flynn* and *Cassidy*. I hope you decide to read them all.

Don't forget, you can purchase eBooks or audiobooks directly from my website will receive a 15% discount by using the code **LauraScott15**.

I adore hearing from my readers! I can be found through my website at https://www.laurascottbooks.com, via Facebook at https://www.facebook.com/LauraScott Books, Instagram at https://www.instagram.com/laurascott books/, and Twitter https://twitter.com/laurascottbooks. Please take a moment to subscribe to my YouTube channel at youtube.com/@LauraScottBooks-wr1xl?sub_confirmation=1. Also, take a moment to sign up for my monthly newsletter to learn about my new book releases! All subscribers receive a free novella not available for purchase on any platform.

Until next time,
Laura Scott
PS: Read on for a sneak peek of *Zeke!*

ZEKE

Chapter One

Sienna Reynolds stopped abruptly when she caught a glimpse of the envelope propped against the front door of her rental home. Just like all the other notes she'd received, her name was written in italic letters followed by an exclamation point. Exactly the way her name appeared on the playbill of her show. *Sienna!*

Turning, she scanned the quiet White Gull Bay neighborhood. At eight o'clock at night, several homes had lights glowing from windows, but she didn't see anything out of the ordinary. She wondered if any had ring doorbells that may have picked up an image of the man who'd left the envelope.

No, she didn't need a camera. She already knew her ex-husband, Josh Allenton had left this note, just like all the others. If not him personally, then someone he asked to do the deed.

Swallowing against a wave of dread, she bent to pick up the envelope, then punched in the numbers on the keypad entry to go inside. She forced a smile when she saw her nanny, Taylor Templeton, sitting in the living room reading a book. "Hi, how was Bailey?"

"A sweetheart as usual." Taylor's brow furrowed when she saw the envelope. "Another one? Really? I didn't hear a thing."

"Yes, but it's okay." She moved to the kitchen to set the envelope on the counter. The note inside would likely be some variation of the previous messages.

I know where you are.

You can never escape.

I'm watching you.

The notes wouldn't bother her so much if it wasn't for her two-year-old daughter, Bailey. She knew Josh had recently decided he wanted joint custody of their daughter, something she would fight against until her dying day.

Hopefully, it wouldn't come to that.

"Sienna, you can't keep ignoring them," Taylor said in a low voice. Her nanny gestured toward the note. "You need to call the police."

"That would be playing right into Josh's hand." They'd had this argument before, and nothing had changed. The moment she called the authorities, Josh would use the information against her. He'd insist on taking custody of Bailey to keep the little girl safe from whatever crazed stalker had targeted Sienna.

No way was she going there. Yet the fact that Josh had found her here in White Gull Bay, Wisconsin, so quickly was concerning.

She needed to do something. She'd returned to her hometown to kick off her solo Christian singing tour, *Sienna!* And while Josh could easily discover she was in the

Milwaukee area, he should not have been able to find her rental home.

Pressing her hands on the counter, she stared down at the envelope. Then she quickly ripped it open. The words were written just like the last ones.

I'm coming for you.

Suppressing a shiver, she shoved the note away. Earlier today at rehearsal, she'd considered calling her brother's best friend, Zeke Hawthorne. If Luke were still alive, he'd have moved heaven and earth to protect her and Bailey.

But Luke had died in a military training mission eighteen months ago. Bailey had been six months old at the time, and Sienna had already started divorce proceedings against Josh after the third time he'd struck her in the face in a fit of anger. The only good thing about being physically abused by her now ex-husband was that she'd been granted sole custody of Bailey.

For now. Unfortunately, Josh was now fighting against that ruling in court. Thanks to his parents' wealth, he had been able to secure one of the best family law attorneys in the state of California. He'd buried her in legal proceedings until she'd wanted to scream.

She knew Zeke was a cop; he'd mentioned working on some sort of tactical team when they'd chatted at Luke's funeral. It was almost as if she could hear her brother in the back of her mind telling her to call Zeke. To get support from someone within law enforcement to fight back at Josh.

"Sienna?" Taylor's voice brought her out of her reverie. "You shouldn't wait until something bad happens. You need to call the police sooner than later."

Taylor had a right to be concerned; her job as Sienna's live-in nanny meant she was at risk of being hurt by Josh too.

"You're right." She blew out a breath and pulled out her phone. She and Zeke had exchanged contact information at Luke's funeral, so she quickly found his name and made the call before she could talk herself out of it.

"Sienna? What's up?" Hearing Zeke's voice in her ear nearly brought tears of relief to her eyes.

"Hi, Zeke, I, um, hate to bother you, but would you have time to stop by? I'm renting a place in White Gull Bay." When he didn't immediately respond, she quickly added, "If you're too busy, I understand. I know this is rather unexpected. If tonight's not good, we can meet up tomorrow or some other day."

"I'm not busy, Sienna. Just surprised to hear from you. I can be there in fifteen minutes, if that works?"

"Perfect, thanks. See you soon." She lowered her phone, hoping she hadn't caught Zeke at a bad time. It had been eighteen months since she'd seen him, and he was likely dating someone or could even be engaged by now. Not married, as she felt certain he would have invited her to the wedding.

Wouldn't he?

"I thought you were calling the police?" Taylor asked with a frown.

"Zeke's an old family friend and a cop." A wailing cry came from the nanny-cam speaker, so she brushed past Taylor to check on her daughter. Bailey was usually a good sleeper even despite the frequent trips from one city to the next.

"Mama." Bailey rubbed her eyes, then lifted her arms. Sienna didn't hesitate to pick her daughter up, cuddling her close. Closing her eyes, she prayed God would keep her daughter safe.

Especially from Josh.

She lowered herself in the rocking chair, holding her daughter while willing her to go back to sleep. After ten minutes, Taylor poked her head into the room. "Sienna?" Her voice was a whisper. "I think your cop friend is here."

"Thanks." Moving gingerly, she rose and set Bailey in the portable crib. Thankfully, the little girl didn't wake up. She left the room, closing the door behind her.

"I'll let you talk to him alone," Taylor said. "And I'll listen for Bailey too."

"I appreciate that." Sienna headed to the front door of the rental, opening it just as Zeke was about to ring the bell. "Hi, Zeke. Please come in."

"Sienna." His broad smile eased her worry. He looked freshly showered, the faint hint of aftershave clinging to his skin. He gave her a one-armed brotherly hug and kissed her cheek. "How are you?"

"Great." She forced a smile, feeling guilty for reaching out because she needed his help. When he arched a brow, she added, "Okay, I could be better. Please have a seat. Would you like a soft drink?"

"No thanks." His gaze was serious now, and he didn't sit on the sofa until she'd dropped into the closest chair. "I sense something is wrong."

There was no point in pretending there wasn't. "I hope I didn't interrupt your evening plans."

"You didn't. I was just finishing up at the gym." Zeke leaned forward, pinning her with a direct gaze. "What's going on, Sienna?"

She hesitated, then stood and quickly grabbed the envelope and note from the counter. Bringing it back to the living room, she handed it to him. "I'm in town for a week and am planning to kick off my first solo tour this weekend."

She grimaced. "I came home from rehearsal tonight to find this propped against the front door."

His scowl deepened as he read the note. Then he looked up at her. "Who sent it?"

"I believe my ex-husband is responsible." She twisted her fingers together. "That's not the first note I've received, and I suspect it won't be the last. My biggest concern is how Josh found me so soon. Bailey and I just arrived yesterday."

Zeke scowled, setting the note and envelope aside. "Maybe you should start at the beginning."

"You probably remember I filed for divorce from Josh," she said. "I told you about that at Luke's funeral. What I didn't mention was the reason I left was because he began to physically abuse me. I had to wait until he struck me hard enough to leave a bruise, then took pictures and went to the police. Thanks to the evidence of abuse, I was granted sole custody of Bailey."

"He hit you?" Zeke's expression turned to stone. "You should have told me that right away."

She sighed. "It's not an easy thing to discuss. Besides, that's not the issue anymore. Josh has a new lawyer and is fighting for joint custody. These threats are his way of paying me back for breaking up our singing duo. After I went solo, I switched to Christian music, which ironically has skyrocketed my career." She'd learned so much about God and faith in the past year. And was humbled by the gifts God had graced her with.

"That's wonderful news," Zeke said, and she could tell he was truly pleased for her. "I'm proud of you."

"Thanks, but God is the one who granted me this gift. And I'm still very afraid of what Josh will do." She bit her lip, then forced herself to continue. "My ex is a manipulative narcissist. I never should have married him, but that's what I get for being young, foolish, and naïve. The point is, he's not one to take my success over his failure lightly."

"I see." Zeke nodded slowly. "We need to call the police to get this note on record."

"No." She rose and began to pace, trying to find a way to make him understand. "Josh wants me to call the police. He wants the entire world to know I'm in danger from some strange stalker. I guarantee that he'll have an alibi for the time frame in question and will act all innocent and concerned, as if he still cares about me."

"But, Sienna . . ."

"No, this is exactly how he operates. This is all part of his master plan." She whirled to face Zeke. "He'll use the perceived danger as an excuse to take Bailey." She used air quotes. "'To keep her safe.'"

Zeke stared at her for a long moment. "Okay, I can understand why you wouldn't want this information to get out in the press, but I have connections within the Milwaukee Police Department. We can investigate this under the radar."

She frowned. "Maybe. But that will only last while I'm here in town, right? My next show is in Chicago. And I'm headed to Louisville after that."

"I see your point." His gaze turned thoughtful. "But that just means we need to find and nail this guy while you're here." Zeke glanced around the rental. "I'll start by sleeping on the sofa."

"What about your girlfriend?" she asked, trying and failing to sound casual.

"No girlfriend or fiancée or anyone special." He gestured to the envelope and note. "We might want to see if we can lift prints off this."

"Don't bother." She was secretly thrilled to know Zeke

wasn't involved with anyone. Not that she was interested in a personal relationship. One bad marriage was more than enough to last her a lifetime. Still, it was nice to know she wasn't intruding too badly on Zeke's personal life. "I had a private investigator do that on the first note about a month ago. There was nothing to find."

"We'll try again anyway," he persisted.

"Only as long as there isn't an official police report that can be used against me." She would not give in on that point. "Seriously, Zeke, I don't want anyone other than you and my nanny, Taylor, to know about this." From this point on, she would not even keep her manager, Dirk Green, in the loop.

"Okay, but my sticking close is bound to raise some suspicions," Zeke pointed out.

That was true. And it was also one of the reasons she was so glad he wasn't involved in a personal relationship. "I know this is asking a lot, but would you consider pretending to be my fiancée? That way you can be here and backstage without raising suspicion."

Zeke stared at her for a long moment, before offering a crooked smile. "I'd be honored."

"Thank you." Tears pricked her eyes, and she turned to quickly brush them away. Oh, she knew Zeke was only doing this because he was Luke's best friend. But she was grateful for his support anyway.

She silently prayed they could get to the bottom of this soon. Before she had to face Josh and his high-priced lawyer in court. The mere idea of being forced to hand her precious little girl over to Josh made her sick.

She vowed to do everything in her power to prevent that.

ZEKE HATED KNOWING his best friend's sister feared for her life and that of her little girl. It made him furious to think about Sienna being physically abused by her ex, and he was determined to make sure the guy didn't get anywhere near her. Or their daughter.

He planned to stick to her like glue. Thankfully, he had his duffel in his SUV, a replacement for the truck that had gotten shot up a few weeks ago. He'd walk the property tonight, to see what he was dealing with.

Tomorrow, he'd talk to Rhy, his boss, at MPD about the situation. When that was set, he'd get Sienna an engagement ring.

Just thinking the words made him flush. Sienna couldn't know about how much he'd wanted to ask her out back when he and Luke were in high school. His best friend had made it clear his baby sister was off-limits. Zeke had honored Luke's wishes, especially since Sienna was way out of his league. Even back then, she'd won several state championships for singing.

Now she was here in Milwaukee, about to kick off her first solo tour.

They weren't high school kids any longer. After everything Sienna had been through, the last thing she needed was for him to mention his former crush on her. He rose to his feet. "I'm going to start by scouting the area outside. I'll need the code to get back in."

"Of course." She rattled off the four digits, then followed him to the front door. "I'll introduce you to Taylor when you're finished. She's my live-in nanny."

He turned to gaze at her. "Are you sure you can trust her?"

"Yes, Taylor's been wonderful. She takes good care of Bailey." Sienna answered without hesitation, but he wasn't about to take anything at face value. Not when it came to protecting Sienna and her daughter.

For now, he'd keep his suspicions to himself. "I'll be back in about fifteen to twenty minutes. Stay inside with the door locked until you hear from me. I won't knock but will call you when I'm finished."

"Okay." She closed the door behind him. He waited until he heard it lock, before moving off the front porch. There was a definite chill in the cool autumn air, and leaves crunched beneath his feet as he moved around the house.

The area was decent, nice homes that weren't sitting on top of each other in a neighborhood with a notably low crime rate. Yet those facts hadn't prevented someone from approaching the house to leave a threatening note on the doorstep.

I'm coming for you.

The veiled threat set his teeth on edge. Resting his hand on the butt of his service weapon, he made his way around the house. The landscaping was nice, but he found himself wishing there were less trees and overgrown bushes. Normally, he'd be impressed by how the owners had created a backyard that provided privacy from the neighbors.

The excess foliage provided far too many places where a perp could remain hidden from view. This early in fall, there were still plenty of leaves on the trees, providing additional cover. Those leaves that had fallen to the ground made it difficult to find footprints as well.

Not the most ideal situation, but not the worst either. He could understand Sienna's desire to avoid hotel rooms. Especially since she was here for a full week. He assumed her first show was Friday but would need to get a copy of her schedule to know the dates, times and locations of each show.

He was surprised he hadn't heard about Sienna's scheduled performances before now. Granted, he'd been knee-deep in several big operations, including one where his fellow teammate Jina had been abducted by a stalker.

Still, he felt way out of the loop.

After clearing the property, he walked to the street to make sure there weren't any cars parked nearby. Finding nothing, he turned to head back, stopping to pull his duffel from the back seat. And his laptop computer. He and the rest of his teammates had gotten into the habit of carrying a change of clothes and toiletries as they often ended up in situations that required an overnight stay. Tonight was proof of that. As he made his way to the front door, he called Sienna to let her know he was coming in.

He found her hovering near the door. Earlier, he'd ruthlessly squashed his instant attraction to her. Now it wasn't nearly as easy to keep his distance.

"Everything is fine." He managed a reassuring smile. "No sign of anyone lingering nearby."

"Thanks for checking." She stepped back, shivering despite her thick burgundy sweater. "I, uh, made up the sofa for you. Sheets, blanket, and pillow."

He nodded, touched by her thoughtfulness. "Thanks. I appreciate that."

"There are three bedrooms." She tucked a strand of her dark-brown hair behind her ear. "I'm in the master with Bailey in the room next to me. Taylor is using the other guest room."

"Sounds good. What about the lower level?" He'd noticed several deep window wells, indicating there was additional living space in the basement. "Mind if I take a look?"

"Oh, sure. The basement is finished off, and there are a few additional bedrooms down there along with a third bathroom if you'd like to sleep in a real bed."

"No, I'll stick to the sofa." He had every intention of being close at hand if someone did try to get in. "I just want to be sure everything down there is locked up tight."

"Of course." Her smile didn't reach her blue eyes. "The stairs are in the kitchen."

She led the way, opening the basement door and flicking on the light. Edging past her, he descended the steep staircase. The ceiling over the stairs was so low he had to duck his head.

There was a large game room, complete with a pool table and dart board. Then he found two additional bedrooms, each with a deep window well leading outside. He understood the need to have the windows with access to the outside in case of a fire, but he didn't like them. He double-checked that those windows were locked, wishing there was a way to secure them better.

The rooms were far enough from the stairs that he couldn't be sure he'd hear the breaking glass if someone tried to get in. He scowled, considering how being here in a rental house wasn't much safer than a hotel room. But this wasn't the time to broach that subject.

Tomorrow would be soon enough.

He mounted the stairs to the main level. Sienna was sitting at the kitchen table cradling a cup of tea in her hands.

"Would you like something?" She eyed him over the rim. "I tend to drink licorice root tea with honey to soothe my throat between performances."

"I'm fine." He nodded to the cup. "Does it work?"

"Seems to." She took another sip, then lowered the cup. "I'm trying to think of the logistics of our arrangement. I know you work during the day, and I'm sure Bailey, Taylor, and I will be fine while you're at work. But if you could give me your schedule, I'd appreciate it. Oh, and I hope you don't mind, but I'll probably have to call my manager to let him know that I—we're engaged." She blushed. "That way he can get the word out."

"You don't want your manager to know about the notes?"

"No." She stared down at her tea for a long moment. "Dirk is a great guy, but he's always pushing me to do interviews and other marketing events. For now, I'd like to keep him in the dark. Thankfully, he has only one TV interview with the Milwaukee Morning show early Thursday."

"Speaking of schedules, I need yours too." The morning show gig was interesting. "And don't worry about my job. I have plenty of vacation time coming. My boss won't mind if I take a week off."

"Are you sure? I don't want to put you out any more than I already am." Her gaze was troubled. "I feel bad taking advantage of our friendship. I just . . . wasn't sure what else to do."

"Hey, there's no one I'd rather spend time with on my vacation," he assured her. He didn't mention his teammates would be shocked to hear about their engagement. Especially since he couldn't tell them it wasn't real. He reached over to take her hand. "Trust me, Sienna. I'll keep you and Bailey safe."

"I know you will." She looked as if she might say something more, but then she pushed her tea aside and stood.

"Good night, Zeke. I'll get you a copy of my schedule first thing in the morning."

"Good night." He stood and waited for her to disappear down the short hallway leading to the three bedrooms. Then he doused the lights and made his way to the sofa. The sectional was soft and long enough to accommodate his six-foot-two-inch frame.

Not that he expected to get much sleep. It took a few minutes to adjust to the sounds of his strange surroundings. The fridge hummed, the ice maker dumped ice cubes into the tray at regular intervals, and a clock ticked with each passing minute.

He must have dozed because a strange sound had him jerking awake. Bolting off the sofa, he grabbed his weapon from the nightstand and moved to the window overlooking the front of the house.

Then he heard the thudding sound again. His heart squeezed in his chest as he softly made his way across the room to the back of the house.

Straining to see through the darkness, he thought he saw a shadow behind the overgrown lilac trees. Then he heard the crash of breaking glass. Swiveling away from the living room window, he ran to the kitchen in time to see the glass scattered on the floor and the brick sitting on the kitchen table.

With a note wrapped around it.

Made in the USA
Las Vegas, NV
20 September 2024

95562044R00134